TRAVELER

TRAVELER

JINN NELSON

ISBN: 978-0-9965840-1-2
First Edition, published by OwlCat Press
Printed in the United States of America
Cover Design: Jinn Nelson
Illustration: Justin Schut
Editor: Morgen Bailey

Books may be purchased in quantity and/or special sales by contacting
OwlCat Press at Books@OwlCatPress.com

Contents

To Lauren
and Liz
and Britt

You saved my sanity.

1

The Catastrophe

The white-haired man sat at the counter with his back to the windows. Through them you could see the station with trains coming and going, tangles of smoke drifting over the heads of waiting passengers. Out there, the smell of smoke and coffee mingled freely with the stench of fish from the fried food stand adjacent to the coffee shop. At all times, the station smelled like a cup of scalded, fishy coffee.

People sought refuge inside the shop, putting off the moment they'd have to go back outside to board the train. They sat or stood around the room, sipping from paper cups and grimacing.

The barista working that day was not one of the good ones.

The white-haired man said nothing about the quality of his drink. He preferred to come in when one of the other baristas employed at the shop was working — when the coffee was good, it was very good — but now it couldn't be helped.

He sipped and glanced at his wristwatch.

Beside him sat a girl in her twenties with blue hair. She had spread papers out in front of her, taking up more than her share of counter space. She tasted the drink the harried barista set in front of her and twisted her lips disgustedly. She shoved back her stool, making it screech, and went to the register where the barista was conducting a transaction.

"This is wrong." She set the full cup down on the counter.

The barista looked at the cup, then at the girl, then at the woman the girl had edged back. Irritated sighs and shufflings rippled down the waiting line.

"Lattes are mostly milk—" the barista began.

"Are they made of burnt milk? This one is."

There were tough customers, and there was the blue-haired girl. Exacting, impatient, easily angered. She ordered a complicated drink, vernacular stuffed with high-sounding adjectives like 'ristretto' and 'breve', a half-pump of this syrup and two pumps of that, and steamed impossibly hot. She tipped well, if one made the drink correctly on the first try. Such a drink was outside this barista's skill set.

"It's steamed hotter than we usually…" The barista trailed off, giving up. "I'll remake it." She glanced an apology at the woman, who smiled tightly then sent a hard look at the blue-haired girl's back.

The barista steamed milk. The waiting line seethed. The girl returned to her stool.

"There isn't time," said the white-haired man without looking at her.

"I know," she said, hovering over her paperwork, "My train leaves in three minutes."

"That's not what I meant."

The girl was confused, but she shrugged and focused on her papers, scribbling notes in the margins and filling in blank lines distributed through the text.

The barista finished the drink and with a victorious flourish set it before the blue-haired girl.

"Just in time. Thanks," the girl said insincerely. She stood and gathered her papers.

"No, I meant you don't have any more time," said the man. "The world ends in—" he glanced at his watch again "forty-eight seconds."

The girl eyed him incredulously, tucked her papers into a satchel and turned to leave.

Instead she staggered as the shop shuddered violently. The cups atop the espresso machine chattered, dishes below the counter quivered on their shelves. The line of customers quieted and turned inward, murmuring to itself.

Another tremor shook the store. The sky flashed white. Not the blue-white of a summer's day, but a white-white. As if someone up there had flicked on a light switch.

People pushed out the doors and spread over the sidewalk, shading their eyes and gesturing upward. A searchlight malfunction, probably, or a solar flare.

"Afraid not," said the white-haired man, as if he could hear their speculations.

The sky then began to melt. It poured down like paint, coating buildings and splashing into the station, covering the trains and platform, and swirling against the shop windows. The barista gasped, setting the steam pitcher down with a *thud* that was covered by her rising scream. Whiteness poured down, consuming more and more of the city. The barista sprinted from the store with the growing throng of exiters, and all were consumed in a downpour of white.

The man at the counter sipped his coffee. Then he set his mug down and frowned at the blue-haired girl pensively, as if at a troublesome mathematical equation. "You should have left with the others. Resistant to compulsion. Hmm…"

She stood gaping at the tide of white climbing the windowpanes, pointing silently.

"It would be a waste to throw *all* of you away," the man mused. "Someone needs to run the shop…"

She found her voice. "What's happening?"

"Your world has ended," he told her. "You're all that's left, I'm afraid. That makes you an endangered species. In fact… you're the only one of *you* anywhere."

"What did you do? Did you kill all those people?"

"Heavens, no. Well, some of them but not the whole world. There was an accident, see. I only just found out this world was about to go, so I hurried over to grab this place."

"Why?"

"I like it. I like to spend time here. And the coffee is good, some of the time." He gazed into his cup. "Now you really should go. I'm about to move this shop and you can't exist in another universe besides your own."

"Where am I supposed to go?"

He raised his eyebrows.

Her eyes widened. She stepped back. "I can't go out there! I'll die!"

The windows cracked, all at once.

The man glanced at them musingly.

"Please! I don't want to die!"

He turned back to the girl. "I can save your life, if you'll agree to run the shop."

The girl only paid attention to the first part of the sentence. "Yes, fine! Please don't let me die!"

"We have an agreement then?"

"Yes!"

The man smiled. "Done. Hold on to something."

The light grew outside, pouring through the cracks in the glass, flooding the room with hot brightness.

The shop jolted, then the whiteness turned to horizontal streaks. A screech like the sound of wheels on metal tracks rose out of the walls, the floor, the counter. Every cup and spoon and coffee bean shrieked. The shriek lasted a full five seconds, and then light and noise and time collapsed into heavy, cold darkness.

2
The End of a World

The train station melted away with a loud fizz.

The people standing outside shimmered, and ceased to exist.

The rest of the planet dissolved into grainy whiteness that faded and vanished like a cloud of steam.

Somewhere in the ether, a cosmic being shrugged and moved on to other experiments — with a sturdier universe, next time — leaving the cleanup to others.

Death was overwhelmed by the billions of displaced, bewildered souls that had presented for transfer ahead of schedule; a rather bad day.

The white-haired man finished his coffee and walked through the closed café doors, to take care of other business.

The blue-haired girl woke in darkness, lying on a concrete floor in the basement of the café.

3

Green Day in Homburg

In Homburg town, which was just waking up and finding that last night's rain had turned into a morning deluge, Jaz Contra stood just inside the open doors of The Defiant, staring into the rainy haze in search of a particular figure. Main Street branched into two streets on either side, forming an awkward wedge where The Defiant stood like a pale ship parting the waters. On a clear day, she could see straight to the field at the edge of town where her new friend, a young Morpha named Bracken, had pitched his tent.

"He forgot, I bet," she muttered, lifting a severely cracked white mug to her lips. She tapped one foot against the black strip separating her floor from the sidewalk. She could send someone to get him, but not before the rain stopped. Jaz scowled at the blurry shapes of pedestrians hurrying toward The Defiant for shelter. "Damn that kid."

Though the air coming in from outside was cold, Jaz lingered on the threshold, letting the nearest pedestrians walk past her into the shop before turning and walking to her place behind the bar. Here it was considerably warmer. Refrigerators hummed beneath the counters enclosing her workspace, and above them on the counter the bronze espresso machine gurgled quietly, its boilers filled and heated. Hot water rumbled in a row of silver kettles on an adjacent counter. Beside the kettles sat a row of clear, vaselike coffeepots with clean white filters in their open tops, ready for fresh grounds. She passed a hand through the threads of steam rising from the kettle spouts, and wiped the moisture on her jeans as she faced the first customers of the day over the counter.

They were green from head to foot.

"Morning," sighed Jaz, stowing her mug on a counter beneath the register.

"Good morning, Jaz," said the first one, pleasantly. "Can you guess who I am?" Her hair and skin were grass green, while her companion was a cool shade of mint. Instead of clothes, their torsos and legs were covered in a scalloped texture that resembled fish scales: a typical shapeshifter response to rain.

Jaz didn't need to guess; she knew the voice. "Astrid. Nice hair."

Astrid pouted, fingering the mass of large green curls that fell to her shoulders. "I was sure you wouldn't be able to guess this time. We haven't had a green day in weeks."

For some months, the local trend in Homburg was to turn oneself a new color each day of the week. Fortunately for Jaz, voice was one feature that most shapeshifters neglected to change. They also had certain favorite patterns that they wore like favorite outfits, which marked them separate from each other and improved Jaz's chances of guessing their identities correctly. It helped, too, that they tended to come into the shop at the same time every day; most of them gave themselves away instantly by ordering their favorite drinks.

Which was how Jaz had learned to identify them in the first place.

Jaz shrugged and said simply, "You always come in with Elisi. Coffee for two?"

"As usual. How did you know Elisi though?"

"I'm a good guesser. And her hair is always straight."

"You can't fool Jaz," said Elisi with a little laugh. "She's half Morpha."

This was partly true — Jaz was hard to fool, but not because she had any shapeshifter blood.

More customers came in, lining up at the counter, and the question-and-answer game repeated itself for the next several hours. Jaz played along because it was expected and it kept them moving smoothly from the register to their tables.

The shop filled with customers in every shade of green, from chartreuse to neon, seeking shelter in The Defiant until the storm passed. They came on foot and riding bicycles, and some even attempting to fly through the deluge. Those on the ground sprouted hoods from their shoulders that curved over their heads, shielding them from the worst of it. From a distance they resembled green humanoid quail. Those in the air moved quicker but had to struggle against sheets of rain pushing down on them.

One of those flying was the elusive Bracken.

Shivering, his featherless black wings trembling with effort, Bracken passed over a group of olive-colored businessmen trundling along the sidewalk and landed in a clear spot outside the café's open doors. He paused to reshape his wings into arms and checked the shoulder straps of his backpack to reassure himself it was still there. Water streamed down his legs to the sidewalk, making a puddle at his feet that seeped toward the floor of the shop.

A slender female Morpha glanced at him as she passed on her way in, then stopped and turned back to him, looking concerned. "You're not green."

Bracken stretched his arms in front of him, confirming they were the same length after reshaping, then rubbed his hands through his wet, black hair. His thoughts were still on the flood waters that had woken him a few minutes earlier, flowing around his head as they beat down the walls of his tent, washing it away along with his food and bedroll. He had barely escaped in time.

"It's Green Day," she informed him helpfully.

Bracken looked down at himself. His upper and lower halves were two different shades of brown and his arms were still black, giving the impression of mismatched pajamas. "Right. I'm not from here. Just passing through."

"Welcome to Homburg then." She smiled prettily. "What brings you here?"

"I'm looking for someone." Bracken leaned to one side to see past her. Customers surrounded the square of counters like grass around a flagstone. Through the gaps he glimpsed Jaz's blue hair as she hurried around, taking orders, making drinks and handing them out.

The young lady stepped into his line of sight. "Human or Morpha?"

"Morpha. My aunt, Sadie." He reached into the backpack for the picture he had brought, but stopped as he remembered it too had been lost in the flash flood. Sighing, he described his aunt instead. The young lady hadn't seen her and was sorry she couldn't be of more help. Bracken, more upset at losing the picture than her lack of assistance, thanked her, flashed a brief smile of farewell, and proceeded to the crowded counter. Two men with wispy, sage-colored beards shifted to make room as he pressed in between them. The espresso machine hummed on his right, dripping espresso into clear shot glasses which Jaz set on saucers and passed to the waiting sagebeards.

"Hey, Jaz." Bracken leaned far over the counter to grab a fistful of paper napkins from a stack beside the machine.

Jaz scowled disapproval of his encroachment into her space. "You're late."

"The field I was camping in flooded." He expected this to soften her, but Jaz seemed to only notice things that affected her directly. Rain that flooded her shop with customers she noticed. Whatever else the rain happened to do outside of the shop earned a shrug at most from the barista. She sullenly dumped coffee grounds into one of the cone-shaped filters in the waiting vessels.

Bracken tried again. "I lost my stuff."

It wasn't technically 'his'. The sleeping bag and cookware had come from his parents' attic, and the camera had sat neglected for years on his older sister's dresser. Bracken had reasoned none of it would be missed. Besides, his sister had a new camera and this old one, a gift from his beloved aunt, deserved a better life than that of a glorified knickknack.

Jaz's hand jerked, spilling water over the counter, and her eyes snapped up to his. "All of it?"

Bracken reached into his backpack and withdrew the boxy camera, which he wiped carefully with the napkins, frowning at the water stains that had already settled into the leather.

Jaz set the kettle down and leaned toward him. "Bracken. The pictures?"

Bracken finished inspecting the camera and set it carefully on the counter. "I'll need a place to stay now, since my tent is gone." He raised his eyes, large and black and pupilless, to her smaller, violet-ringed ones, and tried not to blink. Jaz had a glare that could scorch at a distance. Bracken countered it with a polite, vague expression that he'd perfected on his teachers at school.

"Nice try." Jaz said flatly, and broke away to attend another customer.

Bracken sighed and pulled a brown, rain-spattered package from the backpack. He slid it across to her when she returned.

She brightened. Unlike most Morphas, who smiled even when they slept, Jaz's smile was elastic, put there with effort and snapping back to neutral like a rubber band. "Thanks. I'll pay you in a minute."

The rush turned into a two-way river of customers coming and going. Jaz swept around the workspace, grinding beans, pouring hot water on grounds, tamping espresso, steaming milk, and taking money — all while playing the 'who am I' game with each customer. Bracken lingered at the counter, squeezed between other standing bodies, waiting for a seat to come available.

"What do you want pictures of Homburg for?" He asked as she cleaned and tidied during a lull. "You live here."

"I collect pictures, so what?" She swept a towel over the counter, then went to the register, took several bills from the drawer and dropped them in front of him.

He folded the money and tucked it into the backpack, tying down the top flap with the attached leather laces. "Just curious. It's kind of odd. You could just, go outside and look around."

"I don't go outside. Speaking of odd, you're the only one here who's not green."

"You're welcome." Bracken smirked. She was blunt, even for a human, but he didn't mind. Though she appeared to be in her late twenties, Jaz acted more like a great-grandmother whose old age entitled her to bypass manners. Bracken found that refreshing after living for sixteen years — a lifetime, to him — enduring perpetual, polite smiles from Morpha-kind. "You should open a shop in Cavicea. We don't do color days there."

"No, you have Cabbage Week. With parades and everything." Jaz looked past Bracken, watchful for new customers. Her eyes followed a female Morpha on the sidewalk just passing the windows toward the open door.

Crimson and brown stripes on her upper body set her boldly apart from the backdrop of green pedestrians, and her black hair closely matched Bracken's in shade and texture. "Out of curiosity, where did you get that camera? I feel like I've seen it before."

"It's my sister's, actually. I borrowed it."

Jaz's mouth quirked. "Borrowed."

"…not exactly," Bracken admitted, "But I needed it and she won't miss it. She has a better one."

Jaz looked past him again. "Where is she now?"

"Back home in Cavicea, interviewing cabbage competition winners. She writes for a newspaper."

"Good." Jaz gestured toward the doors. "So that's not her coming in then."

The Morpha in question — a smaller, female, striped, angry version of Bracken — stood in the doorway, scanning the busy room.

Bracken twisted to look and turned back with a strangled yelp. "Kajaani! I have to hide."

Jaz raised her palms and took a step back. "Hey, it's your crime. Don't get me involved."

"I was never here. You never saw me, okay?" Bracken grabbed his backpack and scrambled between full tables to an alcove at the back of the café that sheltered three doors. The center door was padlocked, the right door led to the restroom, and the left had a sign that said 'Employees

Only.' The S in Employees had been scratched out with some sharp implement.

Bracken opened this door and slid through into darkness. He closed his eyes and waited, pressed against the wall, for the door to open. He braced for his sister's hands grabbing him, dragging him out of the shop and back to Cavicea. His grip tightened on the backpack, and the camera inside. Despite his complaint to Jaz about losing his things and needing shelter, he didn't care about either. Tents and sleeping bags were replaceable. The camera, like the aunt who had given it, was not.

Silent moments passed. The door did not open.

Bracken opened his eyes. Perhaps Kajaani had not spotted him after all. Still, just to be safe, he ventured down the stairs to find a more secure hiding place.

The stairs led to a pale brick hallway that turned sharply left. Bracken walked the length of it, passing two doors that were barely visible in the weak light filtering down from the top of the stairs. Further along, the hallway opened into a large, dark basement. Bracken paused to dig into his backpack for his flashlight. The sweeping beam of light revealed the ends of tall metal shelves that stretched toward the back of the basement. Burlap sacks of coffee beans filled the nearest shelves. Bracken took a step toward them, but stopped suddenly. In the corner of his eye he saw a shadow move, accompanied by the sense of a presence.

Someone else was in the basement.

Bracken flicked off the light and quick-walked backward, feeling along the hallway until his hand bumped a doorknob. He turned it instinctively and found it unlocked.

Quickly, he stepped through the doorway, wincing as the hinges squeaked and closed the door behind him, holding the knob and his breath.

Anyone would have heard the door, even if they somehow hadn't seen his flashlight beam. Bracken sensed someone was standing on the other side, about to push in or call out.

Nothing happened.

Bracken decided his mind had played a trick on him. Probably the flashlight throwing shadows on the walls and his anxiety about Kajaani finding him had riled his imagination.

Bracken released the doorknob and turned the flashlight on again. The white beam illuminated a small cot, a full clothing rack, and a desk.

Loose papers covering the desk turned out to be the makings of a book of some kind. There were sketches of birds, and boxy shapes, and a humanoid figure wearing a crown. Several pages were full of neat writing, with sentences crossed out and rewritten, and notes scribbled in the margins. Bracken leaned over one of the pages, lips moving as he read to himself:

*The brown bird flew into the sky
with her new wings, with Fae's
instructions ringing in her ears—*

A chill crept over him, and he stepped away from the desk, sweeping the light around the room until it landed on the cot. The blanket was rumpled and the pillow slightly askew, as if whoever had slept in it last hadn't bothered to make their bed. Dust rose from the blanket when Bracken sat down. Essences of maple and coffee mingled with the musty smell of neglect. Bracken lay back, turned off the flashlight and stared at the ceiling with heavy eyes. Between the rain pounding on his tent all night and the early morning flood, he had hardly slept. Adrenaline ebbed and the darkness relaxed him, making his body feel heavy. His eyes soon closed.

4

The Oncoming Sister

"I was never here. You never saw me, okay?"

Jaz watched Bracken scoot away, then turned to face the oncoming sister. She stalked, rather than walked, to where Jaz stood behind the counter, leaned both hands on the marbled surface and announced, "I'm looking for my brother. His name is Bracken and he stole my camera."

Jaz straightened a small chalkboard menu that Kajaani's hand had knocked aside. "Sorry to hear that. I'll keep an eye out."

"I saw him in here a minute ago," Kajaani insisted. "I'm sure I did. Kid with black hair like mine, with a backpack?"

Jaz shook her head and rewrote the menu with a stick of white chalk.

Kajaani took a step back and turned to scan the room again. "Someone here must have seen him…"

Jaz knew this was very likely. If Kajaani asked customers if they'd seen a disheveled young Morpha with a backpack and a camera, they would most likely report that he had been talking to Jaz for the past half-hour. Not that she cared either way if Bracken escaped his sister, but he had brought her pictures, and he was amusing enough, so Jaz felt more on his side than not. "Ah… what did the camera look like?"

Kajaani turned back to her. "It's kind of unusual. Brown and box-like, with a leather case with a strap. My aunt gave it to me, the last time she visited." Kajaani frowned, the anger rising again. "He's probably looking for her. The only address she ever gave us was in Homburg. My dad even tried to come see her once, but of course the person living there wasn't her. The man who lived in that house knew of her, but said she lived in another part of town. The address *he* gave turned out to be here."

Jaz stopped writing on the chalkboard and looked up at Kajaani, mouth partly open. "Your aunt… lived here."

"Obviously not. People don't live in coffee shops. I *told* him this would happen!" Kajaani banged her fists on the counter top. "He knew what she was like — when we were kids she'd visit on our birthdays and bring presents and tell us these crazy stories, but it wasn't going to last. She never stayed in one place for long. We haven't heard from her the past year. Now he's on some mission to find her, without any idea where he's going or how he's going to get there. Even if by some miracle he *does* find her, he'll be disappointed. She's not the kind of person you can rely on, and she certainly doesn't care about what happens to him."

The chalk fell from Jaz's fingers, bounced off the counter and did gymnastics on the floor before rolling underneath a refrigerator. Jaz bent to look for it, but her mind was no longer on the menu. "Does your brother know, about the address?"

"My dad didn't tell him, fortunately."

Jaz straightened abruptly. "You know what, I think I did see him here earlier. He sold me some pictures. Probably needed money for a place to stay."

Kajaani leaned forward. "Did you see where he went?"

"No, but I'm pretty sure he'll be back. I'd check the hotels nearby, if I were you." Homburg wasn't large. Jaz figured it wouldn't take long for Kajaani to track him down out there, but just in case… "If you don't find him tonight, return here in the morning. He'll probably wander back in."

*

Homburg was a town that turned in early. By ten pm, all of the surrounding businesses were closed, their windows dark. Jaz ate dinner — curly noodles in a sticky fish-based sauce delivered from a nearby restaurant — sitting cross-legged on the counter, the white takeout carton balanced on her knee while she read from a newspaper beside her.

"Quite extraordinary, don't you think? Both of them showing up here."

Jaz shot a dry look at the speaker, a square-shouldered man with handsome human features, sitting on a stool at the counter. He gazed pensively at the wall behind the bar, cheek resting on his raised fist. Black hair streaked with gray slanted across his forehead. "Almost feels planned, doesn't it?"

"Not by *me*," Jaz said pointedly.

The man looked at first inquisitive, then mildly offended. "*I* had nothing to do with it. Trust."

"Excuse me for not taking you at your word. Anyway, Kajaani will find him, or if he returns before she does I'll tie him to a chair until I can hand him off to her. Either way, he's going back where he came from."

The man's mouth quirked. "Do you think so?"

"Positive."

"I thought you might want to see more of them. The boy seems to take after her, at least…"

"I don't." Jaz folded the newspaper and tossed it into a nearby trash can. She hopped down from the counter and searched the shelves below it, coming up with a thin, white hardback book and a sawed-off shotgun.

The man shrugged. He leaned back, stretching long arms over his head. "You ought to use the live rounds this time."

"The blanks work fine." Jaz opened the barrel and saw the chambers were empty. "Just pumping it once stops most people instantly."

"It's your life." The man chuckled as he said this, as if reminded of something funny.

Jaz scowled, shouldered the shotgun and left him, going through the door marked 'Employee Only'. The silence downstairs was heavy, the air cold. She flicked a switch at the bottom of the stairs, flooding the basement with bluish-white light.

Jaz paused at the first door in the brick hallway, glancing at the second door, before entering the first room. It was minimally furnished with a dark wood desk, a bed, a woven rug and a phonograph on a narrow side table. A record with a worn label sat on the turntable. A stack of binders labeled by the days of the week stood on the desk. A thick tome, pages covered in foreign writing, was open on top of the binders. Jaz stared at the page a moment, reconfirming that she had no idea what the writing said. She dropped the thin hardcover on top of the tome and leaned the shotgun against the wall beside the door.

A large framed painting, a gift from a regular customer, hung there at eye level, a depiction of a cliff overlooking a vivid blue ocean. A man stood at the cliff's edge, facing the horizon. His features were somewhat vague, but Jaz recognized him nonetheless: Athamas.

He was the closest friend she had, and also the oldest. He was not a Morpha or a human, or any race that she knew of. He was just Athamas. He was tall and lean and dark-eyed, always wearing a long black jacket with a wide collar over a white shirt. He liked black coffee and blueberry cobbler, and tended to show up whenever both were on the counter. Jaz had often joked that the cobbler was like a reverse calling card that she used when she wanted to see him.

Jaz broke off studying the painting and checked her watch. It was nearly midnight. She went to the bed and fell on it with a sigh, closing her eyes. It was only an imitation of sleep, however. She listened to the silence and counted the minutes passing.

Midnight came, and went.

Jaz opened her eyes. Athamas kept odd hours, and there was cobbler in the upstairs refrigerator. She rolled off the bed and, stepping to the phonograph, set the needle and turned up the volume. Notes of acoustic base and twanging steel guitar filled the room.

> *I hear the train a comin'*
> *It's rollin' round the bend*
> *And I ain't seen the sunshine since*
> *I don't know when...*

Singing along to the music, Jaz found a box of shotgun shells in the corner and slipped a shell into each chamber. Then she threw open the door and stepped out. At the same time, the door to the room beside hers opened. Jaz lurched around, raising the gun.

5

Now Leaving Monday

A series of vibrating notes shot through the room, waking Bracken.

—Twung-twung-twung-TWANG-TWANG-
doom-dumm-toom—

He jumped to his feet. Light showed at the edges of the door, and a shadow moved across the gap underneath. Bracken's breath stopped.

The base notes grew into a rousing song, coming from the room beside him. A steel guitar twanged, the sound shooting through his head like tiny rockets.

Blinking and still unsteady from being so recently asleep, he grabbed his backpack and hurried out the door. At the same time, Jaz stepped out of the door beside his, holding a shotgun. She lurched when she saw him, raising the gun.

He raised his hand, not immediately registering what was in hers.

"Hey. I fell asl—"

Jaz let out a strangled yell. The shotgun boomed.

Bracken shrieked and dropped to a crouch, then threw his backpack up at Jaz's head. She staggered aside, and he scrambled past, galloping up the stairs. He burst into the shop, mind blank, ears ringing. The café was dark, empty. Some chairs were stacked on the tables. Somewhere in the background, water was running.

Bracken sprinted around the tables, hit the doors and streaked into the night.

His feet tangled in something soft and he fell forward, skidding to a stop on a woven rug. He was now in a small, brightly lit room. The steel guitar and bass pounded around him.

—Boom-bum-boom-bum-toom-bum-bum-bum—

He struggled to his feet and spun in a circle, seeing walls covered in photographs, a large painting, a desk, a phonograph, a bed — and a door.

Bracken sprang for it and threw it open.

He was back in the basement.

Jaz stood in front of him, one hand raised to the doorknob.

They blinked, stiffened and yelled in sync.

"Fates!"

"Aagh!"

Bracken shoved past her and streaked up the stairs again, this time knocking over chairs and jumping over tables between himself and the front doors. He hurled himself into the dark—

And smacked into a wall. He fell back, dazed, then pushed himself up, blinking hard. Red spots flecked his vision. He was back in the same little room, with the now-rumpled rug. He gasped heavily and twisted toward the door.

Jaz stood in the doorway, framed by the overhead lights, her blue hair almost standing on end around her flushed face. She grimaced violently and stamped her foot. "Oh, you are *kidding* me!"

"What's happening?!" Bracken shouted back. "Why can't I leave?"

"What—" Jaz pressed her lips together and held up her forefinger. Pushing past Bracken, she went to the phonograph and took the needle off the record.

"What's happening?" Bracken asked again, his voice cracking and ears still ringing. Then, seeing the shotgun still in her hand, he bristled. "You shot at me!"

"You jumped out at me while I was holding a gun," Jaz snapped. "What did you think would happen?"

"I didn't think you'd try to kill me!"

She rolled her eyes. "I wasn't going to kill you. It's loaded with blanks anyway."

"Blanks?" Bracken blinked. "What do you even have a shotgun for?"

"Security." Jaz closed her eyes and breathed deeply before turning back to face him. "Why are you still here?"

"I was waiting for Kajaani to leave."

Jaz's jaw sagged. "In the basement?"

"I… yes?"

Jaz hauled her jaw back up and pointed at the stairs. "There's a sign! Employee only!"

"I didn't mean to stay so long! I was tired and fell asleep."

Jaz threw the gun onto her bed and folded her arms. "Sure. You happened to find your way into *her* room and conveniently fall asleep until after midnight."

"What?"

"You didn't even mention—" She spun away and yelled at the ceiling. "You could have *said* something, you know!"

"I told you about Kajaani when you asked!"

She snapped back around. "I'm not talking about Kajaani!"

"Look, I'm sorry! I just needed a place to stay…"

Jaz breathed in sharply, then closed her mouth and pivoted toward the stairs.

Bracken followed. She went behind the bar and he stood just outside it, watching her. The sound of water he'd heard earlier was from the faucet at the sink. It gushed into a nearly full bucket beneath it. Jaz stuck a silver kettle under the stream, leaving it to fill while she unloaded the dishwasher.

When the kettle was full she set it on a heating element, shut off the faucet and put the rest of the dishes away. While the kettle rumbled, getting on to boil, she set the bucket in a space beneath the sink.

A steaming pitcher of milk sat in front of the espresso machine. She emptied it in the sink, rinsed the pitcher and set it with its mates on a shelf below the machine. She glanced at Bracken, rubbing her hand distractedly through her hair, and wandered over to a counter lined with tins of tea. She pulled a clear teapot from a lower shelf, muttering softly.

Bracken watched her, trying to ignore the tremble in his legs.

"I haven't had to explain this for a while," she said pensively, shaking the leaves in the bottom of the pot.

Bracken sat on the nearest stool before his legs could give out altogether. "Did you make that loopy thing happen?" He gestured in a circle with his hand.

Jaz chuckled briefly. "No. That's the shop. It does that when it resets."

"Resets?"

"Moves to another world."

"Moves to…"

Jaz opened a tin and scooped yellowish leaves out with a silver measuring spoon, dumping it into the teapot. "You know what a carousel is, right?"

He nodded.

"The Defiant is like a carousel. Except instead of it turning and everything else staying put, it stays still and everything outside moves around it."

While Bracken processed this, Jaz lifted the steaming kettle and filled the teapot, then started a small brass stopwatch that was sitting nearby.

Three minutes of silence later, she strained tea into the mug and brought it to Bracken.

He took it, still trying to work up an intelligent response, but only managed: "That doesn't make sense."

Jaz poured some tea into a cracked mug which she took from atop the espresso machine. "Okay — The Defiant is like a train. It goes along a sort of circular track, stopping at seven points along the route, like a train at stations. Only instead of stations, The Defiant stops at different worlds. We left yours at midnight."

Bracken turned to the windows. The panes were black, as if they had been painted over, giving the impression that The Defiant floated in limbo. Bracken shivered and turned back to his tea. He looked up from the mug cradled in his hands to find Jaz watching him. "Train stations," he said, regurgitating the last thing he remembered her saying.

She nodded. "Yeah. Seven. The Defiant stays in each place for twenty-four hours and then goes to the next. So the good news is, we'll come back to your world in a few days."

"So I'm only trapped temporarily."

She nodded again and sipped at her tea. "Yeah. Just a week. When we come back to your world you can leave the shop like normal and go back to your life of crime and photography."

"…right."

"Looking on the bright side, you get a reprieve from your sister for a week." Jaz yawned and set her cup down. "I need to rest for a couple of hours before we open. You can stay in the spare room while you're here."

"Thanks." Bracken sipped the tea. "Whose room was it, by the way?"

Jaz didn't seem to hear him. She rinsed the teapot, returned it to its shelf below the counter, then crossed the workspace and turned off all but the small lights over the counters. "You'll like where we're going tomorrow. Tuesdays are fun."

"Tomorrow is Friday."

"In your world it is. The Defiant runs on a separate time schedule. Your world is Monday. Tomorrow's Tuesday." She saluted him with her raised mug. "Welcome aboard."

*

Bracken returned to his room and sat on the bed. For a long time he stared ahead at a rack of old clothes against the wall, occasionally sipping his tea. The room wavered in and out of focus, as thoughts raced through his mind. In his search for his missing aunt, an inter-dimensional coffee shop was certainly not what he'd expected to find.

His emotions raced with his thoughts; fear and anger at the idea of being trapped there, when he could be in Homburg tracking down his lost relative; wonder and incredulity that he had been transported along with the shop to another world, if Jaz were to be believed. Every so often his thoughts and emotions took a break from racing, allowing the room to come back into focus. Bracken found he was staring at the clothing rack, and at one blue jacket in particular. It had a wide collar and a patch of a brown bird sewn on the sleeve.

With a sudden realization, he stood and crossed to the rack, still holding the teacup in one hand. He lifted the coat with his other hand and held it up. A numb, breathless sensation came over him. The mingled scent of maple and coffee coalesced with the texture of the jacket between his fingers. A memory surged forward: sitting on Sadie's lap, his cheek pressed against the wide lapel of her jacket, listening to her tell a story.

Bracken backed up until his calves bumped the edge of the bed, and sat down heavily, clenching the jacket in a tightening fist. The dust everywhere, and the stale air of the room told him Sadie hadn't been there for a long time, but that wasn't important right now. She had been there. How fortunate that Kajaani had showed up and caused him to seek refuge in the basement. Bracken felt a surge of affection and gratitude toward his older sibling. And Jaz! He'd never suspected that the barista who bought photos from him had also known his aunt.

He fell asleep wrapped in the jacket, compiling a list of questions to confront Jaz with in the morning.

6

Plan A

Jaz woke grudgingly at four am, wincing at the desk lamp she'd left on. She scowled at it, blinking, then at the weekly calendar tacked at eye level on the side of the desk. Beneath Tuesday was written 'Pucheon,' in permanent marker. Below that in erasable marker was scribbled 'Aton, bank. Joli, trowtov.' She relaxed the scowl and rolled out of bed. She retrieved a black vest from the floor and put it on over the mauve shirt she was already wearing. The shirt, her black lace-up boots and blue jeans were the same clothes she had been wearing since the beginning.

She went to the door, had a thought, and picked up the thin, white, hardback book that she'd brought downstairs the night before and left on top of the pile on her desk. She stared at it musingly, then tucked it under her mattress. Then she went out, locking the door behind her.

Glancing to her right, she saw no light coming from under Bracken's door. She stood debating whether she ought to wake him and explain as much as possible before the day began, or just lock him in his room until the following Monday. She wasn't good at explanations, and anyway, there wasn't time. Hopefully, the shock of finding himself in another world would keep him quiet and out of her hair.

Turning left, she climbed the stairs and stepped into the darkened, sleeping shop.

Orange night-lights mellowed here and there, splashing the counter and espresso machine with subdued color. Jaz turned up some white lights above the bar and the workspace brightened around her. It was a six-sided corral of counters and shelves, each counter being its own prep station. The longest facing the front of the shop had the espresso machine, grinders, register and a pastry case. To the left was the drip coffee counter with pourovers, presses and siphons. To the left of that was the tea counter with its own kettles and clear glass teapots on the shelves underneath. Two counters to the far right were empty, and customers usually occupied the stools along both. One more counter along the back wall had extra condiments and brown bags of coffee beans. In the middle of the corral was a rectangular island with a small but mighty dishwasher beneath a ceramic sink.

In a routine that was part personal and part opening for business, Jaz left the mug beside the sink, nudged the waste bin into its crevice between two cabinets, turned on the faucet and shoved a kettle under the cold stream with one hand. When the kettle was full she set it on a heating element at the pourover station.

Five minutes later, with a cracked coffee mug filled with The Defiant's signature Breakfast Blend roast beside her and a box of peach cobbler on her lap, Jaz sat on the condiment counter with her back against the wall, heels up on the adjoining countertop.

Dawn's purplish light grew steadily brighter, lightening the brick plaza outside which was situated in the business district of Pucheon. Five buildings surrounded it, facing each other: The Defiant, the city bank which was currently closed due to an unfortunate smelly slug infestation, a tall office building housing the law firm of Tingle, Shicktin and Vool, a train station, and a small second-hand shop that limped along, refusing to be converted into something more suited to a growing, self-conscious city.

At this hour, no one stirred in the other buildings, and the brickwork plaza was empty of pedestrians. Jaz forked pensive mouthfuls of cobbler, watching the bank.

At three minutes to six, she leaned over to a small radio and clicked it on. Peaceful flute and xylophone music flowed from speakers affixed to the walls.

At two minutes past six, the bank rumbled, shuddered and crumbled inward like a deflating soufflé. Gray waves of dust rolled across the bricks. Bits of shrapnel plinked against The Defiant's window panes, none large enough to cause any damage.

Sirens added discordant notes to the flute and xylophone music as emergency vehicles sped toward the spreading dust cloud that choked the plaza.

Jaz refilled her coffee.

7

Welcome to Pucheon (Please Wear Pants)

"What happened?" Bracken emerged from the basement, backpack hurriedly slung over one bare shoulder, blinking sleepy eyes at the grit swirling against the windows. He was used to seeing Main Street stretching to the edge of town, lined by two-storey buildings. Instead, there was a brick plaza surrounded by the bases of much taller buildings, one of them recently collapsed into rubble.

"Anarchist attack," Jaz reported, settling casually against the wall and lifting the half-empty box of cobbler with her non-mug hand. "Aton Vidersnak just blew up a bank."

"And… where are we?" He felt sluggish and disoriented, like someone jolted awake on a train to find they'd arrived earlier than expected. Questions about Sadie evacuated his mind, replaced with new ones about the world he was now in.

"Tuesday. Pucheon," Jaz answered, eying him with a smirk. "Nice outfit."

Bracken glanced down at himself. In his hometown it was common to 'block,' with large areas of the body covered in contrasting colors and textures. Bracken's version of blocking was to divide his upper and lower hemispheres into dark and light earth tones, sometimes throwing in aqua if he felt festive. Currently, his arms and torso were his natural gray-blue skin tone while his hips and legs were dark brown. He looked like a boy wearing only his pajama bottoms, which he more or less was.

Bracken shrugged and made his way to the nearest stool. "Get a lot of bombings in Pucheon?"

Jaz shrugged. She hopped off the counter and dropped the box of cobbler on the counter in front of him. "I have to open the shop in a minute. You should go back downstairs."

"Why?"

"Things are going to get weird."

"Weird? How?"

Jaz sighed impatiently. "They just will. I don't have time to explain."

"Is there going to be another attack?"

"That's the only one, as far as I know."

Bracken raised his eyebrows. "As far as you know?"

Jaz gave an irritated growl. "I said I don't have time to explain. Just, go downstairs for now. It'll be… better."

Bracken reached over the counter and picked up a fork from a basket of spare cutlery. "Is that what you tell everyone who gets trapped here?"

"No, I put them to work," she snapped.

Bracken helped himself to some cobbler from the box. "I can work."

Jaz glanced at the clock above the doors, shaking her head.

"By the way," Bracken said after swallowing, "who stayed in that room last? I found some clothes and drawings…"

Jaz froze for a moment, a strange muddle of emotions crossing her face. Bracken took another bite and smiled innocently, his cheeks bunching.

Jaz went to the register. Reaching beneath the counter, she retrieved a stained, battered notebook and tossed it at him. Bracken caught it just before it slid into his lap and thumbed it open, adding a smear of peach to the coffee stains on the first page.

"S-this?" he asked around a mouthful of cobbler.

"It's notes on how to make coffee. You'll want to keep it on you while you're working." Jaz opened the cash drawer as she talked, needlessly counting the bills.

Bracken skimmed the notebook while he ate. The first several pages were handwritten in black, sketchy cursive and made no sense to him *(24 oz, 48 g. Add 720 g water. 96 C. #7 gr? Spro dissolved solids 1:2 ratio?)*, while the pages toward the middle were neatly written in pink and blue: instructions and notes surrounding diagrams of brewing vessels and other coffee implements.

Some pages seemed to be collections of miscellaneous notes. The first few were written in neat, loopy cursive:

Even though a certain coffee contains the same flavors, your palate will interpret them differently at varying strengths.

———

If Pucheon's citizens do one thing well, it's commenting on current events. With the exception of emergency workers and bank shareholders, Pucheon's citizens love individuals like Aton Vidersnak who, every time a building goes up, will knock a few down in the name of chaos. Without these destructive types, life would perpetually be Business as Usual, and there are only so many topics to cover when nothing goes wrong. Train schedules, childbearing, expense reports, the boss's incompetence, and the overpricedness of coffee can only carry a conversation along so far before it expires into silence, forcing one to return to the work they had hoped to postpone.

The style and penmanship varied from page to page, sometimes a page long, others just an abrupt sentence or two:

> *The concept of alternates isn't relevant to Jaz*
> *except to note that they exist and she happens*
> *to not have one.*

—

> *The deck outside is a landing pad. You get*
> *hourly rushes and everything must happen fast.*

These ones didn't make much sense. Further back in the notebook, the notes gained headings that seemed to have nothing to do with coffee, like 'Ninjas' and 'Tigers'. Some were written in a different language. Bracken flipped back to the middle pages, which at least had friendly illustrations. He lingered over a page titled 'Brewing Methods'. A small headache quickly formed between his eyes.

Jaz took his sudden quiet as nervous shock. "Just do your best. I don't expect you to learn everything in a week."

"Okay." Bracken closed the notebook, deciding to come back to it later.

"And while we're at it, come learn the register," said Jaz. "You'll take orders and I'll make the drinks."

Bracken carried the notebook to the cash register. It was an old machine with wood sides and rows of gold buttons standing across its wide face. Jaz tapped a button at the bottom of the right corner and a drawer sprang open under the counter.

Bracken picked up a stack of bills from the tray. "What kind of money is this?"

"Jingian currency. It's not complicated. The bills on the right are highest, lowest on the left. Coins are in dimensions of marks and half marks. They mostly use paper here. I keep the prices as simple as possible because counting change wastes time. And we don't take any denominations larger than twenty-five."

Bracken set the stack of bills back in its slot. "So does every day… place… have its own currency?"

"Yeah." Jaz shut the drawer and ripped away the receipt that rose up from a thin slot near the top of the register, crumpled it and tossed it into a small trash can at their feet. "I keep a cash tray for each day and stick it in after midnight."

"Why after midnight?"

"That's when the shop resets." Jaz glanced again at the clock above the front doors. "You don't need to think about that right now. The important thing is that you learn the menu so you can seem like you know something when you're taking orders. Customers are canny. They can sense ignorance and they'll get squirrely if you don't know what you're about."

Bracken smirked. "Squirrely?"

Jaz leaned against the counter and looked past him to the worn notebook he'd already forgotten about. "Keep that handy. It has just about everything you need to know. Most questions can be answered with it. If you get something that's over your head, refer it to me."

"Reference notebook and refer hard questions to you. Right. And what do we do about that building that just exploded?"

Jaz shrugged. "Pour the coffee. That's all we do."

"You don't think the city will shut down or anything?"

"No city shuts down completely. The emergency workers out there will need a caffeine break eventually. They'll want somewhere to rest and recharge. The spectators will want to come inside and gawk more comfortably. Trust me, we'll stay busy enough."

"You sound like you've been through this before."

"Wait until you see what's coming on Friday. This is small beans compared to some of the stunts they pull in Langston." Jaz crossed the room to the doors, unlocked them and flipped a laminate sign hanging on the right-hand door to 'open.' "Now, grow some pants. You look like an advertisement for spandex."

"Spandex?" Bracken smirked, watching her.

"It's something humans wear as clothing."

"I know what clothing is…" Bracken's voice thinned as two short, blue-skinned females wearing wool skirts and blazers materialized from the fog and entered the shop. Both had straight black hair to their shoulders, combed smartly back from their blue foreheads and powdered with gray dust.

"...they should have known he'd do it while the committees argued about fumigation bids," one was saying.

The second coughed lightly. "The trains will be delayed. I'll have to reschedule my lunch meeting."

"Forming a committee about the cheapest way to get rid of slugs. I mean, really. They were just asking for it."

Their voices were unusually high, like a record played at double speed. They clipped up to the counter, which was level with their foreheads.

Bracken giggled, and they both looked sharply up at him. Glowing stars shone in the center of their black irises. Bracken's giggle snagged in his throat, changing to a surprised gurgle. The Jingians likewise took Bracken in, mouths limp and eyes staring.

Biting the inside of her cheek, Jaz snagged Bracken's elbow and hurried to the basement door, dragging him along.

"I'll be with you in a moment," she told the Jingians over her shoulder, opening the door and pulling Bracken through. She held it open a few inches to let light fall in across their faces.

"It's like Blue Day out there," Bracken said as they faced each other on the top step. "Did you see their eyes?" His own dark eyes stared glassily above his smirking mouth.

"It's not Blue Day, it's Tuesday and *you have to wear clothes*," Jaz said in a low, steely voice.

"They have *stars* in their *eyes!* Glowing stars!" Bracken's smirk stretched into a grin. "With six points! I don't think I could even do that!" He started to try.

Jaz gripped his shoulders. "Focus, kid. Pants. Shirt. Shoes. Don't scare away my customers. There's a lot happening today, if you didn't notice."

The white stars forming in Bracken's eyes faded and he straightened his smirk. "Did you help blow up the bank?"

"No. Well… only a little."

"Why are you blowing up banks? Your shop could have been demolished if something went wrong."

"No, it wouldn't. Now listen—"

"How could you help blow up a building if you can't leave this one?"

"There are these slugs in Langston — Friday. They thrive in dark quiet places like air ducts and they smell really bad. I got some to Aton and he used them to clear the building, then he just went in and did his stuff while the bank managers formed committees to haggle with pest control companies about fumigation. This city and its committees. Anyway—"

"You're a smuggler. An inter-dimensional slug smuggler." Bracken looked at Jaz with new respect. "That's kind of amazing."

"It's not a side business or anything. I sometimes get people things they need by unusual means. It's necessary to my own plans. Now—"

"You have plans?" Bracken folded his arms, narrowing his eyes shrewdly. "Are you plotting to rule the universe?"

Jaz shook her head. "No, just escape this purgatory at some point. *Listen*. You need to make yourself look human so you don't cause a panic."

"Why do I have to look like a human? I want to try looking like the blue people."

"After they just saw me drag you in here looking like you do? They'd never buy it. And you couldn't behave like them anyway. You know nothing about their ways. I'm going back out there. If you come out appearing as anything other than a human wearing anything less than pants, shirt and shoes I'll lock you in your room until closing time."

"Fine," Bracken conceded, figuring he could try out the star-eyed look later. "I can texturize."

"Do linen or something. Right now you look like you're wearing spandex pajamas. It's disturbing."

"Spandex is clothing," Bracken quipped as Jaz stepped out.

"Only on Fridays," she said over her shoulder.

8

Memory Tea

After a few minutes, Bracken emerged from the basement 'clothed' in a muted green shirt and reddish pants, cotton in texture. He had also taken the blue coat from the clothing rack in his room and donned that.

After he had reshaped his proportions slightly smaller, it fitted rather well. He walked into the workspace on shoe-shaped feet and stood beside Jaz, who was preparing a pourover vessel for brewing. When she glanced up he gestured at himself with a snarky grin.

She pointed at her own eyes, then at his which were still wholly black.

He concentrated briefly. White appeared around the edges of his eyes, then dark brown irises and black pupils.

"That's great. Thanks." She meditated on the coat a moment, forehead crinkling. "You look like… some kind of art deco portrait."

Bracken was sure she'd been about to say something else, but she turned away and started the coffee grinder before he could ask her about it, or what art deco was.

A star-eyed, cerulean female swaggered into the shop, a white grin splitting her face. She wore a bright green blazer and matching skirt, and a gold watch chain made a curved line from a buttonhole to a small pocket at her waist. Her black ankle boots tapped smartly on the floor and her leather purse swung jauntily from one hand.

"Well," she said brightly as the grinder's ecstatic scream ended. "Well, well, well, eh?"

Jaz dumped the grounds into a waiting cone filter. "I told you Aton would do it."

"Did he ever," Joli chortled loudly. She climbed onto a stool across from where Jaz was pouring, hooking her heels over the crossbar. "I'd like to give him a medal. Between the bank managers scrambling to reassure the account holders, the employees tied in knots about the future of their careers, and all the trains delayed, the city doesn't know what to do with itself."

Jaz poured water over the grounds until they were saturated. Chocolate-colored liquid dripped from the cone and smeared the bottom of the clear vessel. "He's dropping in later. You can shake his hand."

"I will." Brimming with goodwill toward all, Joli turned her grin on Bracken, who was pressing a fist to his mouth to suppress his laughter. "Hello. You must be another relative of Jaz's."

"Another relative?" Bracken lowered his fist and glanced at Jaz. She was watching the water level in the cone go down.

"I don't know what else you'd be. Not many humans in this part of the country," said Joli.

"Right," said Bracken. "So you knew about the bombing too?"

"Jaz notified me." Joli beamed at her again, swiveling on her stool like a searchlight.

"Right." Bracken nodded. "And why is this guy…?"

"Aton Vidersnak," Joli supplied with reverence.

"Why is he blowing up banks?"

Joli turned up the volume again, her voice reaching the highest register yet. "So I can build my garden."

Bracken winced; Jaz just nodded and poured.

"Anyway, that's what it will come to once he hears my proposal," Joli continued. "I don't know what attracted him to this particular bank. Possibly the location, but then again possibly nothing besides its existence. You can never tell with anarchists. When I heard about his scheme I was simply thrilled."

"Thrilled," Bracken said, wincing, "about a bombing."

Joli waved a small hand. "The bank was empty, of course. I had been telling Jaz what I wanted to use the space for, and she set me up with Aton, and now here we are."

"Aton is a regular here," Jaz said. "I just suggested they talk."

"The wonderful thing is that my father is looking for a place to build one of his horrid cafés," Joli chuckled, "and when he finds out he missed this prime location he'll simply weep."

"That's a bit harsh," Bracken said, taken aback. Morphas never openly rejoiced in misfortune, deserved or not.

"Of course it is," said Joli. "He hasn't missed a business opportunity like this since I was seven. Some misfortune would do him good."

Bracken leaned to Jaz. "Isn't she a little young for all this subterfuge?"

Jaz made a derogatory noise in her throat. "They're not as young as they look."

Joli drew herself up, gaining nearly a half-inch. "How old do you think I am?"

"Uh…" Bracken thought she looked about twelve, but he tried to guess high. "Fifteen?"

Joli's cheeks took on a bruised look as she blushed, smiling. "Fifteen was a long time ago. I'm so flattered."

"I'm sixteen," Bracken said.

"He's adorable, Jaz."

"Take him with you," Jaz said.

"So you want to plant a garden in the middle of… what town is this again?" Bracken asked.

Joli blinked. "You must be from the sticks, not to know Pucheon."

"I live pretty far away," he agreed.

"Where?"

He tried to say 'Cavicea' but couldn't push a sound out past the first letter. "C— c— c— c—"

Jaz set down the kettle and watched him, openly amused.

He tried again, only managing to stutter and click like a typewriter.

"What's wrong with him?" Joli asked Jaz, keeping her eyes on Bracken.

"He fell," Jaz answered smoothly. "On his head."

Joli tskd sympathetically.

"His brain might be damaged. It's too early to tell. If he talks nonsense ignore him. I'm just looking out for him until his family can find him and take him home," Jaz said.

"No," said Bracken, trying to correct Jaz's story, "I'm tr-t-t—" He couldn't say 'trapped'. He tried a few other sentences. He tried saying he didn't belong to this world, that Jaz had pulled him into another dimension or whatever she had called it, and that he wanted to go back home immediately. "I don't b-b— She— she-t-t— I want to go— I-I-I-AHH!" He pointed desperately at the windows. "That's not Main Street and everything is wrong!"

Some nearby customers looked over, their star-eyes staring.

Joli shook her head sadly. "Poor thing."

"Poor me," said Jaz, "I'm stuck with him."

Bracken clenched both fists and turned on her. "Jaz! What happened?"

"He has some memory loss too," Jaz continued, blandly absorbing his look and passing a full coffee mug to Joli.

"Memory loss," Joli echoed with sympathy, as if hearing the story of an abused kitten. Her smile reappeared abruptly. "Lucky you, I have votwort stashed nearby." She jumped down from the stool and hurried away across the shop, leaving Bracken stuttering a protest. The table of onlookers went back to their conversation.

Jaz took his arm and pulled him close. "You can't talk about The Defiant to these people. They don't know."

"What, I can't say I've been kidnapped into another dimension?" He could say it all right now, when no one was listening.

"Who we are. What this is. You can't say it. But I guess you figured that out."

Bracken pushed his face closer to hers. "What are you doing to me? Why are you doing this?"

"I'm not doing anything. I told you, I'm trapped here too."

Bracken wasn't sure he believed her. She had been so amusedly watching him stutter and panic a moment earlier. But then, last night she had said she was also trapped, and she seemed somewhat relieved to say it. In fact, she'd called The Defiant purgatory, but Bracken hoped that was an exaggeration.

"This should be enough for a cupful," Joli's siren-like voice was heard before she was seen climbing onto the stool. "It's not much but it should bring something back for you."

She produced a long, clear tube topped with a cork that contained several crimson, fernlike leaves floating in vermilion liquid. Jaz procured an empty mug and Joli uncorked the tube, pouring the liquid into the mug.

"Joli is a horticulturist. She works with plants," Jaz explained to Bracken. "She's the best in the country."

Joli smiled. "Oh, now…"

"She supplies me with sweet herbs and spices for specialty drinks. Mint, cardamom, cloves, nutmeg, ginger—"

"Actually, ginger is a root." Joli pushed the mug toward Bracken, stretching her short arm as far as it would go across the countertop. "Drink this."

Bracken stepped back. "I don't—"

"Drink," said Jaz, like a mother enforcing manners on an unruly child.

Bracken sipped and tasted hot peppers. His tongue burned though the liquid was cool. Rather than spit the brew over the counter, he swallowed quickly. The tincture seared his throat as it went down.

"I have trowtov for you, Jaz," Joli said, dropping the empty tube in her purse.

"Don't get them mixed up," said Jaz. "I need the anti-memory stuff." Her gaze went past Joli's shoulder to the windows, habitually checking for new customers. "Joli… your father…"

Joli spun to look and gave a little shriek, like helium escaping a balloon. Bracken stifled another giggle, his eyes watering from the strain and from the spicy tea.

"He's already scoping out the property. I'd bet on it. He'll do almost anything to get a space on the plaza for one of his horrid pie shops." She twisted back to Jaz. "You didn't mention to him I was coming here, did you?"

"Of course not!" Jaz looked offended. "I only order from his bakery, and I don't even talk to him directly. I want you and Aton to make your deal. I wouldn't sabotage that."

Bracken tried to follow their looks to spot the father, but he was hidden among groups of females clustered on the sidewalk.

"Aton can be fickle. If he sees a business mogul like your father hanging around he may split. Or start a fight. You never know with him. You need to get rid of him before Aton shows up," urged Jaz.

"I know." Joli gathered her purse and hopped off the stool. Bracken and Jaz had to lean over the counter to see her. Joli waved and hurried to the doors, heels tapping double-time. She squeezed out past two customers coming in, muttering a scant apology as she passed.

9

Clandestine Photography

Bracken pushed the mug of tea toward Jaz. "What does votwort do?"

Jaz took it automatically, staring at the street through the windows.

"Jaz?"

She blinked and refocused on him, leaning close again. "Listen. I need your help with this. Aton will arrive soon and I need to keep him here until Joli gets back."

Bracken sighed. "What do you want me to do?"

"Just take orders for me."

The two new customers, both female, approached the register. They wore hard hats and a light coating of concrete dust. One stared down at the little chalkboard menu beside the register and the other gazed into the pastry case.

"I need espresso," said the first one in a voice like a tired squirrel, still looking past Bracken. "A latte. Four shots. What flavors do you have?"

Bracken tried not to stare at their eyes. "You mean syrups?"

"Yes."

"We have…" Bracken consulted the coffee manual. "Vanilla, caramel, and chocolate."

She lowered her eyes slowly to focus on him. The white stars shrank to pinpoints. "Do you have pomegranate?"

"Uh…" Bracken looked to Jaz, who pressed her lips together and shook her head. "No. Sorry."

"Vanilla then, I suppose." She paid and dragged herself to a stool to wait. Jaz steamed milk.

Customers entered in small groups, and Bracken did his best to parrot their orders to Jaz. The language was confusing. Certain words had several meanings, and most drinks had variations that didn't make much sense to Bracken. 'Black coffee' meant either coffee brewed in a brewing vessel or extracted as espresso from the espresso machine. Some customers said coffee when they meant espresso, and some said espresso but meant anything else. A few customers who initially ordered espresso left with herbal tea. Bracken learned by trial (the drink he thought was being ordered) and error (the drink that Jaz had to make after the first was returned in dissatisfaction) that cappuccinos could be made hot but not cold, and that iced coffee couldn't be warmed by adding hot water.

He was relieved when the last customers walked away with their orders and he had a moment to breathe. He opened the notebook to the middle and read the names of various combinations of espresso, water or steamed milk, paying attention this time.

"Jaz," he said after a few minutes, carrying the notebook over to where she stood at the espresso machine, "whose handwriting is this? It looks familiar."

She looked up from watching espresso drip into a shot glass, glanced at the page held out to her, and then at him with the same forehead-crinkled expression she'd given his coat earlier. "I don't know. I don't remember."

Bracken didn't believe her. "Jaz, c'mon—"

At that moment, the doors opened and Jaz looked eagerly over the espresso machine to see who it was. "Oh." She gave a little gasp and pressed her hands to her hips. "That's Aton. Watch the register. I need to talk to him and make sure he stays until Joli gets back."

Bracken looked at the person who had just entered. His jaw slackened. "That's him?"

The person weaving through the scattered tables was as effeminate as Joli, though his hair was gathered at his neck in a neat tail and he wore short pants instead of a skirt, and black leather loafers.

"Yeah," said Jaz. "Don't make a scene."

"He looks like a girl!"

"That's the kind of scene I'm talking about." She lowered her voice as Aton secured the stool recently vacated by Joli.

He waved three fingers toward Jaz, requesting four shots in a voice that could have belonged to a grandfather chipmunk.

Jaz started the grinder.

Aton met Bracken's stare with eyes identical to Joli's. "Who's this?"

Jaz looked up from tamping grounds in a portafilter. "My cousin. Bracken. He's helping out today."

"Are you sure he's not a corporate spy?"

"I interrogated him thoroughly," Jaz assured him.

"At gunpoint," Bracken added.

Jaz set a white cappuccino cup half-full of espresso and a small glass of sparkling water before Aton, waving aside his money.

"For the tip jar then." He pushed it toward her and took a sip of coffee. "Interesting. Nutty, yet floral…"

Jaz nodded. "I'm working on a backwoods theme for autumn."

Bracken scoffed quietly.

"What?" Jaz set a fist on her hip and shot him a narrow look.

"Autumn-themed coffee. It's… you know…"

"He's not a very good employee, Jaz," Aton observed.

Bracken shrugged. "I'm not really an employee. I'm just visiting."

Aton leaned toward him, squinting. "From where?"

"Ah…" Bracken turned to Jaz, who looked like he'd just poured iced coffee over her head. "Home?"

"And home is?" Aton's squint deepened.

"Bracken." Jaz thrust the tip money at him. "Put this over there."

She didn't specify where 'there' was and Bracken didn't ask. He took the money and slunk away, taking his backpack to a table by the windows.

As he sat, his vision flickered.

The shop became a living room with a red armchair beside an open window. The scene through the window was half blue sky, half blooming flowers. It was the garden in his backyard at home—

Bracken blinked hard and rubbed his eyes. Customers sat at the tables nearby, sipping from coffee cups, talking, or staring out the windows. All of them were petite, blue Jingians… except for a tall human with gray-streaked black hair, who sat alone at a table, gazing out the windows.

Bracken nodded to himself. He was definitely in The Defiant—

The room flickered again and was replaced with another memory.

Two slippered feet rested on the coarse red and brown rug in front of the same red armchair. He lay on his stomach near those feet, his cheek pressed against the rug. A smaller, younger Kajaani lay on her back beside him.

Her dark eyes reflected two spots of yellow lamplight, her hair spread in flat waves around her head, listening to the story being told to them.

"Once there was a brown bird who loved to fly. She decided to leave home and fly to a new land she had never seen, beyond the great Snowy Mountains…"

Bracken lifted his cheek, imprinted by the frayed rug fibers, and turned his head to look at his younger sister, Riva, who sat cross-legged against the couch with a potted purple plant corralled in her lap, brushing the umbrella-like leaves with her fingertips…

Then a brief snapshot of a lazy, bright summer morning around the breakfast table; a knock at the front door; a scraping, scrambling race to be the first to answer it…

He was sitting on his aunt's warm lap, resting against her shoulder and watching her face as she looked out the window. She was telling him more about the king of tricksters, her voice and eyes unusually serious.

"Fae hides behind many masks. That's why the bird didn't recognize him at first. Once she did, of course, it was too late. She was already trapped."

"But she escapes in the end, right?" he asked in his high child's voice.

Sadie stared thoughtfully out the window. But instead of answering, she looked down at him with a grin. "I almost forgot your presents. Go get your sisters…"

He was looking at Kajaani's forehead and ears sticking out around the boxy black camera as she pressed the viewfinder to her eye; she snapped the shutter as fast as she could at Bracken and Riva while they chased each other in circles around the rosemary bushes…

He was lifted by Sadie into the umbrella-shaped leaves of a tall purple plant; pulling white pods loose with his own small hands, then standing in the shade munching the sugary pods with Kajaani; crunching granules between their molars and showing each other their purple-stained tongues…

He was standing at the end of the driveway in a cold downpour, waiting and watching for Sadie to arrive; Kajaani's arm settling around his shoulders, muttering angrily about Sadie's unreliability; shadows obscuring the empty road; stars glimmering in a cool night sky and Kajaani's arm still around him…

After that, the memories seemed to lose power, fading back into their usual place in his mind's eye and letting him become aware of where he was at present. A few more recent memories resurfaced, but a line had been drawn between the colorful memories before the driveway and the dull, ordinary ones after, when childhood ended and life ceased to be interesting.

Bracken blinked and looked around the café. Effeminate Jingians were still scattered around the spacious café, seated at tables with cups, books or newspapers. The tall human was gone. A few patrons stared blankly out the windows: the dust outside had thinned, diminishing into a dirty haze through which policemen, firemen and other concerned citizens could be seen inspecting the damage.

A smile slowly grew on Bracken's face. Unzipping his backpack, he retrieved the camera and snapped a few pictures of the demolished bank across the plaza, some of the other customers, and then a couple of Jaz and Aton talking at the counter. Aton glanced Bracken's way as the shutter clicked.

In another moment, as Bracken lowered the camera, Aton was off his stool and halfway to the doors. Jaz followed after, delayed by having to come around the counter. "He's no one, Aton, I promise."

"He's most likely been bribed. I know when I'm being stalled."

"Joli is going to be here any minute, she's just running late."

"If she still wants to make a deal she can meet me here at a time of my choosing. And please abandon any attempt at clandestine photography in the future. If my picture ends up in the paper it'll be impossible to get anything done."

And then Aton was gone, his head bobbing just above table height outside the windows as he walked quickly to the corner and out of sight.

10

Don't Blame Me

Jaz stood at the doors watching Aton go, chewing the inside of her cheek. Then she shifted her eyes toward Bracken.

He shuffled his feet under the table. "So... what just happened?"

Jaz marched over, white-faced, and grabbed the camera out of his hands. "What were you doing?"

"I just took a couple of pictures..."

"He thinks you're a corporate spy!" She lobbed the camera back at him.

He fumbled to catch it. "Hey, be careful—!"

"Do you know how hard it was to gain Aton's trust? How much bloody espresso I've donated to his caffeine habit? How hard it was to get those stinking slugs for him?!"

Clutching the camera to his chest, Bracken ventured a guess. "...really hard?"

Jaz slapped both palms on the table and leaned toward him. "You just killed two goddamn months of planning!"

Two Jingans near them looked over, ceasing their conversations. Jaz straightened, breathing heavily through her nose.

"I'm sorry, Jaz." Bracken stowed the camera safely in his backpack. "I didn't realize it would spook him. He's walking around in public, I thought…"

Mouth tight, Jaz turned and stalked back to her workspace.

After a moment, Bracken followed. Jaz slumped over the condiment counter and banged her forehead down several times on the marble. Then she clenched her head in both hands and pulled at her hair, dry sobbing through clenched teeth. "Sucking milk burning son of a cake eater…"

Bracken stood in the gap between the tea counter and the wall, shifting his weight from foot to foot.

Jaz sighed deeply and lowered her hands from disheveled hair. "Should have locked him in the frothing basement. I should have."

"Can't we explain it was a misunderstanding?"

"I tried, but I can't tell him who you are and he knew I was being evasive."

"We can tell him the camera film got destroyed."

"I don't know when he's coming back. Might be next week, might be next month." Jaz crossed to the grinder. She grabbed a thick paintbrush from a basket beneath the counter and vigorously cleaned grounds from the chute.

"There goes that brilliant plan."

Bracken did some mental math and came to a sobering realization. "By next month, do you mean by our time? Or his?"

Jaz's jaw tightened. She slapped at stray grounds on the counter, sweeping them onto the floor.

Bracken swallowed. If seven days in Pucheon were seven weeks in The Defiant, then thirty days equaled over six months… "Couldn't Joli build her garden somewhere else?"

"Yeah, but I needed Aton's explosives for tomorrow." She threw the brush back into its basket.

"Explosives?"

"My reward for getting him the slugs and keeping quiet about it." She shot a narrow look at Bracken.

"Oh…"

"So that's taken care of!" Joli's voice on the other side of the counter made them both jump. Her head and shoulders rose into view as she mounted a stool, grinning.

Jaz's return smile was her briefest yet. "You're back…"

"Yep." Joli was flushed, her cheeks and forehead purple. "We don't have to worry about my father anymore. I took care of it."

"Uh-huh. Um…"

"It was brilliant. I pretended to be waiting for a train, and we went for brunch, away from all the dust and noise. He started to tell me his plans for buying the property and putting up one of his horrible pie shops. I feigned interest, enough to keep him going on so much that he didn't notice I slipped trowtov in his tea. By the time we finished our frittatas, he couldn't remember ever *drinking tea*, much less his plans for extending his franchise onto our turf." Joli chortled in her throat, like a purple chipmunk villain, rubbing her hands together.

Jaz stood very still, both hands clutching the edge of the counter. "How much did you give him?"

"All of it! I wasn't taking any chances. He'll take a few days to recover and by then we'll have our deal all wrapped up!" Joli looked into Jaz's graying face and ceased her hand rubbing. "Of course, I have more at home. I'll bring it for you tomorrow."

Jaz's knuckles turned white. "Tomorrow will be too late."

"Too late for what?"

Jaz made a slight choking noise. "Never mind."

Joli shifted on her stool and inquired about Aton.

"He didn't make it," Jaz said after a moment.

Joli gaped. "What? Why not? Was he captured? Murdered?"

"No. He stopped in for a minute but couldn't stay."

"But… I can't support this venture on my own. His finances are the key. And if my father talks to the realtor and finds out I haven't bought the property yet he'll snap it up like the business thief he is."

"Give me until tomorrow," Jaz said after another pause. "I'll get him back."

Joli's face returned to a more serene blue, and she nodded. "Call me the moment he comes in."

"I will."

Joli looked at Bracken and smiled consolingly. "Hope you recover those memories. I'll bring more votwort tomorrow."

"Thanks," Bracken murmured.

Joli took her leave. Bracken and Jaz retreated to the back counter where they stood side by side, leaning against it.

"And there goes my plan for Friday," Jaz muttered, shaking her head. "Super."

"How will you get ahold of Aton by tomorrow?" Bracken asked.

"Tomorrow for Pucheon is a week for me. I have some time to think about it." Jaz turned and slumped facedown on the counter. "There goes that plan. Shaz is going to kill me when he finds out I don't have the explosives."

"Who's Shaz?"

"I'll tell you later." Jaz picked herself up and wandered over to the espresso machine.

11

Infinity Box Blues

Customers suddenly multiplied, coming in all at once as if someone had scattered vouchers for free drinks across the city. In reality it was simply afternoon, when Jingians grew tired after lunch and needed a pick-me-up. On this particular day, their exhaustion stemmed from the trauma and activity surrounding the demolished bank.

Bracken made an effort to stay behind the counter, taking orders to help Jaz in the hope he might redeem himself. But he was also tired, and Jaz was sullen and snappish, so he soon slid out of the workspace and escaped to a corner table.

He folded his arms on the tabletop and rested his head on them, watching the activity in the plaza. He was sorry about what happened, but it wasn't his fault that Aton was easily spooked. And Jaz hadn't said not to use the camera. In fact, she had barely told him anything before shoving him behind the register. He hadn't asked to be her helper. He hadn't asked for any of this.

The more he thought about it, the more irritated he became. If he were outspoken like Kajaani, Bracken would have yelled back at Jaz when she yelled at him about the camera. Kajaani's response to confrontation was to confront it right back; Bracken's was to pretend it didn't exist. Internalize. Seethe quietly until the bad feelings faded away and the trouble passed.

He sat and seethed through the afternoon and into the evening. His eyes slowly closed and he slept, head down on the table, until a tap on his shoulder startled him awake.

It was dark outside. The plaza was brightly lit by iron street lamps that curved down at the top like thin black plants, their lights like hanging buds casting circles of light onto the dusty bricks.

Bracken blinked, his reflection coming into focus in the windows. Jaz stood beside him.

"I got us dinner." She walked away before he could answer.

Bracken pushed back his chair and stretched. The café was empty except for themselves. The sign beside the doors was turned to 'closed.' The clock above the wall read eleven forty-five.

Jaz hopped onto a stool at the counter. "You eating or not?"

Bracken walked over to the counter. Dinner was an assortment of white takeout boxes clustered on the countertop. Jaz had one open already. She pushed another toward him. The warm smell of seared meat and vegetables tempted him, and he took it, along with the fork she held out. A hesitant bite revealed the meat was generously coated with a sticky sauce, seasoned with what Bracken assumed was black pepper. The taste awakened his stomach, which had been empty for too long.

He ate quickly, scooping up large forkfuls, standing at the counter. Jaz was quiet on her stool, eating more slowly.

"I'm not good at explaining things," she said after several minutes. "When you spend all your time in one place, doing the same things every day, you forget about the details that make up the routines. They're just part of you. Part of life."

This made sense to Bracken, but he was still a little angry at her. Enough to say, after swallowing, "It's not that hard. You could have told me about the blue people, and the bank, and Aton being neurotic."

Jaz made a noise in her throat, almost a short laugh. "I did tell you."

"Only as it all happened."

She stirred the food in her carton. "You try it sometime. No, tell me now. Tell me all about Cavicea."

"You know about Cavicea."

"Pretend I don't."

Bracken thought. "It's bigger than Homburg. There are more streets and parks and houses and stuff—"

"No, I mean details. What exactly were you doing before you left? Every day?"

Bracken had to think. "I went to school. Mom would make us breakfast sometimes. I stopped going because I wanted to find Sadie…"

"But what was happening? In detail."

"…nothing happened. Just everyday stuff. Eating breakfast, going to school, coming home…"

"Now who's vague?" Jaz smirked, then grew serious. "It's the same here. The daily patterns. Morning rush, afternoon rush. Evening crowd on certain days. The difference is, I've been living these patterns a long time. Long enough that I can't remember it all. I don't have enough room in my mind for all the memories I make."

She reached over to a binder sitting on the counter. It was thick, the cover stained brown from coffee spills. Across the front and along the spine it was simply labeled 'Wednesday.' "I record things that happen each day in these binders. So I can recall details. Past events, people. Stuff like getting slugs for Aton and arranging a meeting between him and Joli."

Bracken stared at the binder. It was at least three inches thick, and small bits of colored paper stuck out here and there, marking certain pages. "How long have you been here?"

Jaz swallowed a mouthful of food before answering. "Longer than I'd like."

"How come you can't get out?"

"The Defiant is like a train, right? Except with this train you can only get off at the same station you got on. The home station."

"You don't have a home?"

"It's gone." Jaz tilted her carton toward her and poked at the contents with her fork.

"What happened to it?"

"Ceased to exist."

"How?"

Jaz shrugged, stabbing the vegetables but not eating them. "The day my world ended, I was here in this café, sitting at the counter. I don't remember what I was doing there. This guy with white hair turned to me and said something like, 'Sorry to inform you, but your world is about to disintegrate.' And then… it did."

"All except for this place."

"He said he liked it, so he saved it."

"Why did he let you live?"

Jaz frowned. "I asked him to. But in exchange, I have to run this shop."

"Where did he go?"

"I wasn't sure, for a long time. First I had to find out what he was…" Her face became still, almost expressionless, her eyes distant. "Eventually I tracked him down to one of the worlds The Defiant visits. Thursday. He's there, somewhere. I just have to find out where, and get a message to him. Get him to come here and free me."

Bracken held his carton of congealing meat and vegetables between his hands, watching Jaz with widening eyes. The memory of lying on the rug beside Kajaani, listening to his aunt's stories when she came for one of her rare visits, came back again. "This place is… it's like an infinity box."

Jaz's forehead crinkled but she said nothing.

"My aunt used to tell us stories about a princess who got trapped by an evil king inside an infinity box. It kept whoever was inside from leaving, so this princess has been living her whole life inside this box…"

Their eyes met over the takeout boxes.

"And the princess had blue h… oh…"

Jaz's eyebrows twitched upward into her blue bangs.

"Oh." Bracken sank back in his chair and said it a third time. "Oh."

Jaz sighed, glancing up at the clock above the doors.

Bracken straightened, shoving the box away from him. "I knew it! She *was* here! You lied to me!"

"What? I didn't lie to you."

"You didn't tell me she traveled with you!"

"I couldn't tell you anything, just like she couldn't tell you anything!"

Bracken wished he hadn't moved so quickly. His legs wanted to fold under him. "All the stories she told us. The ones we thought were fairy tales. The princess and the infinity box. The brown bird and the trickster king. Tuoni the raven. The North Wind. They were about these… worlds or whatever they are."

Jaz glanced at the clock above the doors again. "Something like that."

Bracken clutched at his head, dragging his fingers through his hair. "So the camera…"

"Came from Langston."

"The ink pen she gave to Riva?"

"Grayson's Gulch, I think," Jaz said, tapping the Wednesday binder. "We'll be there tomorrow."

"The candy tree?"

Jaz smiled briefly. "From Joli, of course."

Bracken turned and leaned heavily against the counter, staring at the café reflected in the windows. The streetlights were only just visible beyond the reflection. "She told us she traveled. We thought she meant around the country, but… Holy bugs. I should have guessed…"

It was easy to imagine his energetic, eccentric aunt Sadie traveling in The Defiant. She would breeze into town three times a year with new presents and stories about the princess in the infinity box, or the brown bird, or Tuoni the raven, and breeze away again, not to be seen again until the next year. His family hated that about her. She was too flighty, too different.

That was exactly what Bracken had loved about her.

Bracken's focus shifted to himself in the windows' reflection. He still wore his human disguise of pants, shirt and shoes. And of course, the blue jacket that had belonged to Sadie. Now here he was, on the same adventure she had taken.

He smiled at his reflection. "So, where is she now?"

Jaz pushed the binder along the counter to him. "Find the most current page and read it. I'll be back. And switch off the faucet please."

As Bracken turned toward her, she vanished.

12

'Round Midnight

Chairs all around the room flipped upside down and landed loudly on their tables. Cups shifted on the shelves. The brewing vessels quivered. The dishwasher door fell open. The rag bucket that usually sat on the floor under the espresso machine was now in the sink, about to overflow beneath the abruptly gushing faucet.

Bracken swiveled left and right, looking tensely around. "Jaz?" He leaned forward, peering over the counter, but saw only the floor. Nothing moved besides a haze of steam rising out of the dishwasher, and water overflowing the edge of the bucket, splashing into the sink.

Bracken turned a circle, searching the room. "Jaz?"

The basement door opened and Jaz stepped out. She frowned and went to the sink, shutting off the faucet while closing the dishwasher door with her foot.

"Where did you go?" Bracken asked.

"I told you the shop resets at midnight." Jaz nodded behind him at the clock above the door. The hands pointed up at twelve. "That includes me. At least, physically."

"You didn't say how."

Jaz shrugged. "That's how."

Bracken folded his arms. "You really need to work on your explanations."

Jaz moved to the counter where the espresso machine sat and picked up a silver pitcher of steaming hot milk that hadn't been there before the shop reset itself. She pulled a shot of espresso into a mug, poured in the milk, stirred in some chocolate syrup and handed the mug to him. "Fine. At midnight everything in the shop reverts to its physical location at the moment it became... whatever it is now. I 'restart' downstairs in my office."

"Why in the office?"

"There wasn't always an office. I built that part later. And added a bed. I got tired of landing on concrete. Right, so that's what happens at midnight. Let's move on to tomorrow."

She tapped the front page of the open binder.

Bracken stared at her a moment. He went to ask another question, but then shrugged and read aloud. "Grayson's Gulch. Country: Zunghar. World:... X-I-O. Exio. Exo."

"It's pronounced Zhow."

"Huh. I guess they wouldn't call it Wednesday, would they?" Bracken sipped the drink she'd handed him. It was chocolatey and warm, with an underlying bite from the espresso. "Mmm. This is good."

"Glad you approve. Xio has weeks just like everyone else. Seven days long. Twelve months in a year. Today is Saturday, for them."

Jaz pulled a monthly calendar from a pocket in the front flap of the binder and set it on the counter, tapping the appropriate date. Then she went into the dining area and turned the chairs down onto the floor.

Bracken read a note taped to the calendar. "Blaise, formula, high noon. What's high noon?"

"It's an expression they use for midday. Blaise is coming in to pick up his formula then," Jaz said from across the room.

"Why do you have it?"

"I don't, yet. Shaz does."

"Who's Shaz?"

"Shaz Shef — it's all in the manual. Just read."

Bracken found a page titled 'People of Interest' and then located Shaz's name, which had this notation:

Unofficial sheriff of Grayson's Gulch. Works for Mei Grayson. Runs mining enterprise in the quarry. Blight on face of civilization. Tiger.

Bracken twisted toward Jaz. "Shaz is a tiger?"

"Yeah. Xio has talking tigers. I was going to trade with him for the formula but since I don't have the explosives from Aton, I'm going with plan B."

"Which is?"

"Accuse Shaz of stealing the formula and threaten to ban him from the shop unless he gives it back."

"What's this formula for, exactly?"

"Tiger repellent."

"What?"

"Tiger rep—"

"No, what is it?"

"It's a smell tigers can't stand. Right now you have to wear it in a diffuser. Most people keep them around their necks or attached to a watch chain or belt. The diffusers can break or fall off though. A guy named Blaise invented a formula that's injectable and permanent, which would be a huge boost for humans. Repellent is expensive, and it's also a good business. Tigers aren't exactly brilliant but they're born for extortion and intimidation. Shaz's boss, Grayson, owns the nearest repellent factory. And the quarry. And the whole town, basically."

"So… the tigers sell a smell that repels them."

"Not just sell it — they control it. They decide who gets repellent, and when, and for how much."

"Sounds like a racket."

"It is. The humans have to go along with it because it's the best defense available against becoming tiger food."

Bracken cast a glance at the doors. "What happens if the tigers get in here?"

"They come in all the time. They usually behave in here. Usually."

"Tigers come to a café? For what, milk?"

"Milk, tea, coffee… Shaz is a steady customer. Gets a heavy cream latte."

"They don't attack you?" Bracken turned a page and found several photographs tacked to the paper. A few were of humans. The others…

"No. Occasionally. If they get angry enough. But it doesn't happen a lot. They need someone to make their coffee. Even if a tiger could comprehend the science behind coffee they couldn't make it like I do."

Bracken touched one of the photos that didn't contain humans. "Right… but according to this picture they do wear clothes."

"Mostly hats, sometimes waistcoats. They don't dig pants."

"Can't blame them." Bracken yawned, resisting the fatigue of a long day. "So you're aiding the human revolution by getting this formula back from Shaz and giving it to Blaise without Shaz finding out what it really is."

"Exactly."

"And you're going to do this by intimidating Shaz — a tiger — into handing it over."

"Hence the shotgun, yes."

Bracken smirked as he raised the cup to his mouth. "Sounds like dangerous fun."

"More dangerous than fun." Jaz set the last chair down and came over to him. "I'm used to them, and it's true that they don't usually attack humans inside the shop. But they're still tigers. They can and will kill you if you make them angry enough. So be careful not to make them angry."

"Got it."

"I'm taking a risk confronting Shaz. He likes my coffee, but… you know. He's a tiger."

"Has he attacked you before?"

"Not in a long time. It should be okay. It'll be okay. If something goes wrong though, run downstairs and stay there until midnight. You should be okay if you lock yourself in my office."

Bracken set his mug down on the counter. "You're saying 'okay' a lot. It's not as reassuring as you might think."

"I just want you to understand that you need to be careful not to tick him off."

"I get it. Don't tick off the tigers." He lifted the mug nonchalantly and took a sip, raising his eyebrows at her.

Jaz nodded. "Great. I'm going to bed. Wash your cup when you're done."

"Jaz?"

She glanced over at him as she moved to the basement door.

Bracken unconsciously tightened his fingers on the mug's handle. "Why did Sadie travel with you? Was it an accident, like with me?"

Jaz's forehead crinkled, and she scratched at the back of her neck while considering her answer. "She was… sorta hiding from her brother. Your dad. Apparently, they didn't get along."

If Bracken had had a human heart, it would have sunk at these words. Instead he felt just a tightness forming in his center. "It wasn't that they didn't get along, he just… didn't understand. He wanted her to be with the family, and make a life in one place. Like most of us… most of my kind do."

Jaz shrugged and continued to the basement door. "You and she are kind of alike."

Bracken perked up at this. "We are?"

"Yeah." Jaz pushed the door open and started through it. "You think The Defiant is some kind of escape hatch."

"What is it then?" Bracken called after her.

Jaz's voice floated back through the closing door. "A trap."

13

Grayson's Gulch

Bracken woke on his cot several hours later. He vaguely remembered finishing his drink alone — staring at Wednesday's binder but not really paying attention to it anymore — before finally going to bed.

It had taken a while to fall asleep. His body was vibrating from caffeine, his mind refusing to quiet. It felt as if he had lain in the dark, staring at the ceiling for hours, before finally drifting off.

Bracken stretched both arms overhead, yawning deeply. He could hear Jaz moving in the next room. He sat up on the edge of his bed, rubbing his eyes, then went out. Jaz's door was open. She stood at her desk, her back to him, open on the top of a heap of binders, tapping the barrel of the shotgun against her shoulder.

"Do you ever sleep?"

Jaz turned, startled. "You're up…"

Bracken's vision kept going fuzzy. He rubbed his eyes again. "What time is it?"

"Five." Jaz glanced back at the book. "We'll open in about an hour."

Bracken went in and looked over her shoulder at the tome. Crisscrossing black lines formed a pattern like badly woven cloth on the yellowed pages. The gaps between the lines widened and narrowed at random, marked here and there by occasional squiggles.

"What's that?"

"It's a history book."

Bracken squinted at the page. "It looks like… scribbles."

"That's Sassacus script. It's written with both hands. Apparently, the technique takes about ten years to master but it's also the most accurate way to record something you want to remember. If it were a video recording, it would also have historical notations embedded in the picture, and notations on the mental states and personalities of anyone present."

"You can read that?"

"No. You have to have a Sassacus scribe read it. And they don't often come here."

"How did you get it?"

"I borrowed it from an elf."

"With permission?" Bracken wiggled his eyebrows.

She smirked. "Yes."

"What for?"

"You remember that guy with the white hair I told you about, who trapped me here? I tracked him down to Thursday's world, and I think this book can tell me where he is, exactly."

"And if you can find him maybe he'll let you out."

"Yeah. First I have to translate the book and get his location, but that's the bottom line. Yeah." She closed it gently and led the way upstairs.

The windows of the café had gained translucency with the dawn, revealing a gray, grassless gulch, pebbly on the bottom, with long, irregular stripes of shale up the sides. The rim made a dark line across the whitening sky. Some buildings — glorified plank shacks — stood along the base of the ragged incline. A few brightly painted wood signs hanging above the weathered doors indicated the presence of a general store, a drug store, a shoemaker and a butcher shop.

Bracken was drawn to the windows, staring up at small flames hovering in the gray sky. They blinked on, then off, then back on again, like fireflies. The sky continued to lighten, revealing that the flames belonged to giant balloons with baskets hanging beneath. The balloons themselves were various colors: bright yellow, crimson, muted green. A few were striped or checkered. They glowed faintly when the flames flickered on, the colors seeming to pulse with light.

"What are those?"

The windows vaguely reflected Jaz in the workspace, stowing the shotgun below the register and opening a bag of coffee beans. "What do they look like?"

"Giant balloons."

"There you go."

Bracken pressed closer to one of the windows. "What are they doing out there?"

"Traveling." Jaz measured some beans and ran them through the grinder. "Humans get around here by balloon or bi-plane. It's safer than traveling on land when you have to go more than a few miles."

"Do the tigers sell those things too?"

"Some of them." Jaz deposited the grounds in a brewing vessel and watered them with a slow, thin stream from the kettle. She went into the kitchen, came out with a pastry box containing blueberry scones, set it on the counter and then finished brewing the coffee.

Bracken came to the counter and hopped onto a stool. "Is this Grayson's Gulch?"

"Yep."

"It's just some shanties and a gravel road."

"Yep." Jaz poured the coffee into a café mug for Bracken and her own cracked one, opened the pastry box and lifted a scone to her mouth. "Wait till you see the townsfolk."

After they ate, Jaz unlocked the doors and continued the opening preparations: writing the coffee of the day on the menu board with chalk, filling gas burners beneath a row of brewing vessels that looked like hourglasses on brass stands, restocking paper filters for the vase-shaped pourover vessels, stocking milk and cream in the little refrigerator beneath the espresso bar.

Meanwhile, Bracken slouched over the counter by the register, his attention more on the windows than the menu he was supposed to be memorizing. Every few minutes a balloon bumped gently on the rocky ground between the barren hill and The Defiant, released two or more passengers, and silently drifted upward again while the former occupants strode with purpose to the doors. Once inside, each group paused, glancing at each other and letting out the breath they'd been holding during the trek across the road. The sun's hazy light behind the travelers made their faded, long-worn clothes seem shabbier than they were. The men straightened the long lapels of their suit jackets and brushed dust from their trousers. The women shook out their floor-length skirts and checked their hair with tiny round mirrors produced from some fold in their gown ensemble. Each traveler wore a silver pendant that gave off a pungent, minty-smelling perfume.

Bracken quickly learned that Black Coffee was the drink of choice in Grayson's Gulch, which the travelers and townsfolk camped at tables around the room ordered by the potful. They preferred the siphon brewing method, a blend of science and art that was flashy, produced a bright, clean taste, and like their trusty hot-air balloons, its heat source was an open flame.

In most of the other worlds, the siphon was an on-again, off-again attraction, conceding center stage to the classy but sensible pourover vessels and press pots, which made up for their relative plainness with comforting simplicity, but in Grayson's Gulch the siphon dominated.

"It's simple," said Jaz, showing the process to Bracken as she brewed a pot for a customer. "Pour boiling water in the bottom vessel, place it over its burner, fit the top vessel over the bottom to create a seal. The water gets pushed up by steam. When it reaches 198 degrees, grind the beans, add the grounds to the water, stir, saturate, let the grounds rest half a minute, stir again, let it sit another minute, remove from the heat source. The coffee filters out as the liquid is sucked back down. See?"

"The… coffee goes in the water on top and gets sucked back down," Bracken repeated, remembering little and understanding less.

"Yeah, you got it. Easy stuff."

"So, where are the tigers?" Bracken asked as Jaz ground beans for another pot.

Jaz silenced the grinder and paused to glare at him.

The rest of the shop seemed to stop with her and, if they didn't glare outright, hardened their somber gazes.

"Sleeping," Jaz said, clipping past him to a waiting siphon and pouring grounds in the simmering water in the top glass. "Tigers aren't morning people."

"Thank the fates," muttered a redheaded woman to her male companion. They hunched together at the counter over a half-full siphon pot between them, coffee mugs cradled in their hands.

Jaz pulled Bracken's elbow, tugging him behind the espresso machine which hid them from most of the dining area. "Don't mention tigers here before noon. The morning crowd is all human. They're trying to relax before the other half of the town wakes up."

She spoke low, so the folks at the counters couldn't hear her discussing the unpleasant topic, tamping espresso grounds into a portafilter and locking the basket under the top lip of the espresso machine.

"Aren't you waiting for one to come in though?" Bracken asked, watching creamy brown espresso drip into a shot glass.

"Yeah, but they don't need to know about it." Jaz glanced up at the doors and tensed. "Speak of the devil…"

A tiger swaggered in, walking on his hind feet, pushing both doors open with massive front paws. His long, striped tail swayed casually behind him. He wore nothing but a top hat, through which his ears poked up, swiveling and twitching as he scanned the room with golden eyes.

Bracken recognized him from a photo in Wednesday's binder. "Hey, that's—"

"Shaz Shef!" The small man at the counter hissed to his red-haired companion. She grabbed the coffee pot and they abandoned ship, seeking safe haven at a corner table.

14

Plan B

Shaz Shef, the menace of Grayson's Gulch, silenced the room as he crossed it.

"Good morning, Jaz," Shaz rumbled. His voice seemed to come from a quarry inside his chest.

Bracken flinched, awed more than scared. Shaz was easily eight feet tall.

Jaz ignored him, studying the last drops of espresso falling into the shot glass.

Shaz breathed in and snorted out, twitching an ear back. He leaned over the top of the espresso machine to look down at Jaz, like a fox looks into a chicken coop for his next meal. "Guess what day it is."

Jaz lifted the shot glass and sipped. "Wednesday?"

"Mmm," he rumbled. "Funny. It's Saturday."

"If you say so." Jaz took another sip of espresso, as if consuming her coffee might not happen if she didn't down it right away. "I don't have your goods."

"Not as funny." His ears twitched stiffly.

"Good. I wasn't joking. The deal is off. I don't trade with people who steal from me."

The fur along Shaz's neck shifted, subtly rising. "Steal from you? What have I stolen?"

"A recipe. I dropped it on the floor yesterday and you took it." Jaz pointed at his head. "And for some reason, put it on your hat."

Shaz touched a claw to a small, folded piece of paper tucked into a silk band above the broad brim. "I don't know what you're talking about. This is mine. I wrote a… note. To myself. If you were careless and lost something though, it's not my fault."

"Fine." Jaz drained the shot glass, thumped it on the counter and strode to the register. "I'll keep the goods, you keep the recipe and get out of my shop."

Shaz placed both paws on the counter, leaning forward. His fur stood up all along his back and shoulders, and his tail snapped side to side like a whip. "You're pressing your luck, female."

Bracken tried not to stare at Shaz's paws, but he couldn't help it. They took up most of the space between the register and espresso machine.

"Maybe. But I prefer this to luck." She hefted the shotgun and pumped it once. "Now *git*."

She hadn't included the human patrons in the command, but they took the hint and, except for the redhead and her companion at their corner table, trickled out, leaving Bracken and Jaz alone with the growling tiger.

Bracken had never been in a fight before. Cavicea was a relatively safe town with low crime. A family friendly town. Even in school he had avoided bullies with relative ease, thanks in part to his older sister who had a protective streak and a solid right cross. Bracken's personal strategy was to avoid confrontations before they started.

Jaz and the tiger were way past the confrontation stage now.

Prickles of alarm sparked over Bracken's skin, warning — demanding — that he move away. Quickly. To anywhere. Bracken reached out and caught Jaz's elbow, pulling it as he stepped back. Her head flicked toward him, eyes crinkled in brief surprise. "Bracken, get—"

Shaz uncoiled while she was distracted and sprang onto the counter, landing on three paws and swiping at the shotgun with a fourth.

Jaz shrieked. The gun flew out of her hand and skittered across the floor. Shaz launched over the counter, cutting deep scratches across the countertop with his hind feet. Jaz just managed to shove Bracken aside before she went down beneath the full weight of the tiger. Shaz pinned her with one paw on her chest and swiped across her face with the other. Her cheek shredded, deep lines of red splitting her skin. She struggled to move, kicking beneath him. He stamped down with a back paw, digging into her thigh. She screamed hoarsely and punched, hitting his lower jaw. He roared and swept her arm away with one paw, slashing at her throat with the other.

A shotgun barrel slammed into Shaz's open jaws and he rocked back, smashing against the condiment counter. He dropped onto all fours, facing the redheaded woman who had come into the workspace with shotgun in hand.

Bracken had staggered clear and now crouched against a row of shelves beneath the espresso counter, staring at the scene, unable to move or shout or even think. Jaz had gone still, sprawled on her back on the floor, blue hair across her face stained dark purple with blood. One of her arms was trapped under Shaz's paw, pierced by his claws.

The redhead thrust the shotgun barrel toward Shaz, gloved finger ready on the trigger. "Fun's over, fuzzy."

Leather covered her body like armor: brown leather gloves, a long leather duster with reinforced elbows, leather chaps on her legs, and thick boots that laced to her knees.

Shaz snarled, baring his long teeth.

The redhead narrowed her eyes, aiming the shotgun between his.

"If you kill me, Grayson will have you dragged in and chew your throat himself," Shaz snarled.

The redhead snorted. "I'm not gonna kill you."

She pulled the trigger. The gun boomed, quieter than before. A cloud of moisture puffed around Shaz's face. The air sprang to life with the strong scent of spearmint and vinegar.

Shaz yowled. He recoiled, shaking his head and rubbing his eyes with the back of a paw. He staggered around the workspace, yelping and clawing at the countertop, blindly trying to climb over. He failed several attempts, smashing mugs and plates, leaving deep gouges in the counter and shelves beneath.

Red watched with a growing smirk on her pale face as Shaz finally grappled his way over and streaked for the doors, going over or through any chairs or tables in his way.

When he was gone, Bracken found he could move again. He hurried to Jaz and knelt beside her, brushing her hair away from her face. It was a mask of red, blood oozing freely from the gouges across her cheek. Red's companion, a balding, perspiring bloke also wearing a leather duster but without the gloves and chaps, was already there, pressing his hands over a deep cut across Jaz's thigh. Blood pulsed through his fingers, streaming onto the floor in a spreading pool. Jaz's eyes were unfocused, and she breathed in short gasps.

"It's not good," Red murmured, standing over them.

"Call a doctor," said the balding bloke.

Red shook her head. "Too late."

Bracken clutched Jaz's hand. It was cold and gray, and her fingertips were blue. "Jaz? Jaz, don't die…"

Jaz coughed once and did just that.

Bracken released Jaz's limp hand and fell back against the cupboard, feet pulled close, staring at her body and chewing his thumbnail.

There was a long, long silence.

"Sorry for your loss," Red offered quietly. "She was a good sort."

"Thanks," Bracken said dully. One thought kept running through his head on repeat: Jaz was gone, before he could get her to tell him where Sadie was. How could he find her now?

"This your first day?" Red asked.

"Pretty much."

She made a sympathetic sound. "I'll go find the undertaker."

Bracken shook his head. "Not yet." He wasn't sure if Jaz could leave the shop even as a corpse. If she couldn't, there would be questions and an investigation, and having a bunch of people poking around downstairs among the otherworldly items on the shelves and in Jaz's office seemed like a bad situation for someone like himself to be in, who couldn't answer questions anyhow. Packing the shop with tigers and townspeople and carrying them along with him, through the days back to his homeworld, was the only way to show them what was going on, and Bracken didn't want to unleash something like Shaz Shef on the unsuspecting town of Homburg — or any other town, for that matter. "I should clean up first and… and keep the shop open like normal. She'd want that. This place was her life."

Red and her companion helped Bracken carry Jaz downstairs into Bracken's room — he didn't want to risk them seeing the stack of weekday binders and the Sassacus history book on her desk — where they arranged her on the narrow cot and covered her with a blanket.

Red nudged the balding bloke's arm after a moment. "Let's give him a minute." They went upstairs.

Bracken had only seen death once before. It had come to his grandmother, while she sat resting in the armchair by the open window that looked out over the garden, holding Bracken in her thin lap. But that had been a bloodless death, with only a stirring in her sleep and a breathless incoherent murmur — "What are you doing here?" — a quiet exit. The only similarity between that death and this one was the suddenness of it.

With Jaz's death also came screaming and blood, and the guilt of knowing it was mostly his fault. Not to mention the horrid sense of being abandoned. Abandoned, in an interdimensional coffee shop, in a world full of tigers.

Bracken fell back against the wall opposite the cot, rubbing his face with both hands, barking short laughs of hysteria. Being trapped in this wacky café was one thing, but being trapped here alone was something else entirely. Jaz was the only person who knew what to do, and he couldn't ask for help now. And what if he died next?

Well… so what?

At least his end would be interesting. At least Jaz had left him with something different than Cavicea.

At least he would have died trying to find Sadie, which was all that mattered anyway.

Bracken straightened and lowered his hands. He studied Jaz's form, covered with the blanket. Time hadn't stopped, he reminded himself. He'd have plenty of time later to search The Defiant for clues to Sadie's whereabouts.

All he had to do was survive today.

He went out, closing the door behind him, and walked upstairs to see what else could go wrong.

15

Plan C

Red and the balding bloke were standing in the alcove outside the basement door, conversing quietly with their heads together. Bracken walked past them into the workspace. He stared down at the broken glass and blood left from Shaz's visit.

"Time won't clean this up," he murmured. He returned to the basement, hunted down a mop and bucket, brought them out, set the bucket in the sink to fill with water. Then he realized he had to go back into the basement to find a broom.

"We'll help you." The bloke picked a rag from a pile that had fallen on the floor and scrubbed at some blood on the cabinets. "I'm Blaise, by the way. This is my bodyguard, Aja."

"I'm Bracken." Bracken paused sweeping up shards of glass and gave Blaise a closer look. "Jaz mentioned you."

"I come here a lot," said Blaise. "She has the best coffee around. Er, had."

Bracken nodded. The world — worlds — would have to do without Jaz and her coffee from now on.

"She's recovered from some pretty bad wounds before," said Aja, going around the counter to pick up siphon remains. "Guess you can't come back from them all though."

"I guess that's the end of our grand scheme too," Blaise sighed, mopping up a puddle of blood.

"Not now, Blaise," Aja said, out of sight on the other side of the counter.

"You mean the formula?" Bracken asked, finishing with the broom and dumping the contents in the trash can.

Blaise snapped around to face him, the mop clenched in white fists. "She told you about it? What did she tell you? Did she find it?"

"Shaz has it."

Aja's head and shoulders rose into view across the counter. "Shaz?"

"Yeah. She was trying to get it back."

"That's what she meant by saying he stole her recipe!" Blaise interrupted, abandoning the mop and cutting across the workspace toward Bracken. His foot skidded in some blood collected between two rubber mats on the floor.

Bracken grabbed his arm, stopping his fall before it started. "Careful."

"Thank you."

Aja set a cracked siphon vessel on the counter. "Wish I'd known that before I blasted him with repellent. I'd have grabbed it first."

Blaise turned toward her, moving a bit more carefully. "You said he'll come back."

The smirk Aja wore during Shaz's mad escape resurfaced. "I don't mind shootin' him twice. I'd shoot him all day if I could."

With their help, Bracken cleaned away the blood and glass, and set unbroken items back on the shelves. The workspace remained disheveled, the counter was permanently scratched, and a spot in the row of siphons was conspicuously empty, but the shop no longer looked like a crime scene.

"I could use some coffee when you get a chance, Bracken," said Aja, settling on a stool and smoothing open a crinkled newspaper that had been abandoned by another guest. "About a gallon will do."

"Make it five," said Blaise. "She's a bottomless pit."

"Oh, uh…" Bracken looked around the workspace for something inspirational. Coffee involved beans and water and a cup, but beyond that he suddenly couldn't remember a thing. He wasn't so much an employee as an interloper, a customer standing on the wrong side of the counter.

He grabbed the coffee manual, but before he could search the pages, the doors opened and three tigers came in. In the lead was a large male, wearing a brown Stetson with holes cut on either side for his ears. His stripes were somewhat faded, and he ambled rather than stalked, giving Bracken the impression of advanced age. The other two were smaller, but also younger, and instead of hats each wore a ribbon around their neck, tied in a neat bow above the shoulder.

The older tiger in the Stetson stopped in front of the register and looked down at Bracken, expectant.

Bracken stared back.

The tiger made a sound in his throat, something between a growl and a cough.

Bracken jumped. "Hi! Hi. Hi…. hi. Um… what… what can I get you?"

The tiger's ears flicked back, then forward, though his eyes remained fixed on Bracken. "I'll have a cappuccino."

"Really? That has… coffee in it…" Bracken couldn't imagine a tiger drinking coffee, even now. And how did they drink it? Lap it up from the cup? Could they even hold a cup?

"Yes, I know." The tiger's ears came forward, but not in a way that exuded happiness. He seemed… tense.

"Right. Right, sure. No problem. No problem…" Bracken hurried to the espresso machine and stared at it. Cappuccino. That meant espresso and milk and some foam.

Bracken opened the coffee manual, turning to a diagram that matched the espresso machine.

Trying to go by the drawings, he filled a pitcher with milk and twisted a knob on the front of the machine to activate the steam wand as he had seen Jaz do before. The wand screamed, agitating the milk until it boiled over and burned Bracken's hand. He dropped the pitcher, sending a cascade of milk onto the counter and floor.

Now all three tigers were staring, ears forward.

"Ow! Ow. It's okay. I'm fine…" Bracken tried to smile casually. It was hard to be casual with his hand burning and milk pooling under his foot. "Just a little new at this."

He filled a clean pitcher and restarted the steaming process, this time turning off the wand before the milk started to boil. Accomplishing this task without further injury, he set the pitcher down and began the process of pulling espresso. He didn't know why it was called 'pulling', because there was nothing to pull. One unlocked the portafilter from the grouphead under the top lip of the machine, placed the portafilter under the nearby grinder, filled the basket with coffee grounds, pushed them down with a tamper and replaced the portafilter in the grouphead. If anything, the espresso was pushed out by the force of hot water from the boilers, not pulled.

Bracken followed this procedure without incident, then had to decide which button to push to produce the espresso.

There was one button above each of the three groupheads, so he chose the most likely candidate, the one above the filled portafilter. The machine rumbled, grumbled, and for a few anxious moments, nothing else happened.

Bracken's finger hovered in front of the button, about to turn it off and start over, when a dark brown liquid slowly dripped from the portafilter into the shot glass beneath. It moved much slower than Jaz's espresso did, dripping sluggishly for a while before turning into a weak, wobbly stream. Bracken waited, unsure when it would be 'done'. Jaz always seemed to know when to stop the shot, but there was no line on the shot glass, and no indication in the manual about when this should happen.

Bracken shifted from one foot to another, trying to keep from showing concern. The tigers watched him, unblinking. Aja and Blaise also watched, though Aja quickly lost interest and returned to her newspaper.

Bracken waited until the shot glass was nearly full and then pushed the button again to stop the shot. It was done enough. He poured the espresso into a cappuccino cup, then poured the milk. An island of solid foam floated on the milk, and splashed down in a sort of lump on top of the drink.

Feeling elated — he'd made his first drink! — Bracken carried the cup over to the register counter and set it down in front of the tiger with a smile.

All three tigers looked down at the drink. There was an extended silence, after which the older tiger sniffed and said, "It's burned."

Bracken blinked. "It's what?"

"You burned it. Burned the milk, burned the coffee. Burned. I can't drink it."

Bracken glanced at the drink, then at Blaise, at a loss. "I... I didn't realize. I'll make it again."

The tiger breathed out heavily, and his ears flicked backward.

"Or... I can make you something else?" Bracken edged back from the counter, glancing desperately at Blaise.

The tiger's tail whipped to one side. "Where's Jaz?"

Blaise looked at Bracken, then at Aja, chewing his lip. For a moment it seemed he was about to remain with her, but instead he swallowed and came around the counter with Bracken.

"Jaz got attacked by Shaz Shef," Aja said, talking to the tigers without looking at them, "so it's just Blaise and the kid here. Don't expect anything fancy."

The tiger's tail relaxed. He stared at the cappuccino and nudged it away with one claw. "What... else do you have?"

Blaise took the open manual from Bracken as Bracken washed milk from his arms and dabbed a towel over his front. "Press pot," said Blaise after scanning the manual. "I'm quite familiar with that method..."

He trailed off as he turned a page. His brow furrowed as he read silently.

"Is it coffee?" asked one of the smaller, female tigers, the one wearing a green ribbon. The other female, whose ribbon was dark purple, fixed inquiring golden eyes on Bracken.

"I think so."

"You think so?"

"Yes. It's coffee." Bracken nodded.

"We'll take that," the older tiger said, slapping coins on the counter with a directive to keep the change.

"What kind of syrups do you have?" asked the female with the green ribbon.

"We have…" Bracken glanced to Blaise for the manual, but the man was absorbed in whatever he was reading. "Blaise?"

Blaise looked up at him. "What is an alternate?"

Bracken's breath caught. He snatched the manual from Blaise's hands. "Uh, nothing. It means alternate… beans. Kinds of beans." Turning back to the tiger, he said, "We have… vanilla, caramel and chocolate."

"Do you have clorentine?" she asked.

Bracken's forehead crinkled. Clorentine? "I don't think so."

"Cherry?"

"No, sorry." Bracken stowed the manual beneath the register, pushing it far back on the shelf.

"That's too bad. You really ought to have them. Very common flavors." She joined her companions at a table.

"What is clorentine?" Bracken asked Blaise as she left.

"You've never had a clorentine?" Blaise looked skeptical.

Bracken shrugged weakly.

"It's a type of fruit," Blaise answered, measuring out coffee beans with an air of concentration. "Tastes like a cross between citrus and cactus."

"Cactus? I mean, cactus. Right. I remember now. Where I'm from we call them… citrons."

Blaise shook his head. "To each their own. Hand me that press pot."

A press pot, Bracken learned, was very simple to use. One measured grounds into the cylindrical vessel, poured hot water over those, stirred and let it rest for several minutes before pressing the grounds to the bottom with the plunger. Blaise fussed with the grinder, concerned about achieving the proper coarseness. Bracken watched unhelpfully over his shoulder.

"Perfectionist," Aja muttered, turning the page of her newspaper.

"Coffee is an exact science," Blaise told her, sticking his nose in the air and making his already receded jaw merge into one line with his throat, like a lizard stretching toward the sun. The grinder obligingly spit out several batches of coffee grounds before Blaise gave a satisfied nod and proceeded with the brewing and pressing, while Bracken gave instructions from the manual.

When it was ready, Bracken volunteered to deliver the pot and three coffee mugs to the tigers. He set everything on the table and stepped back, lingering nearby so he could watch them drink.

It was fascinating. Their paws, now that he saw them up close, were in fact four separate digits: three fingers and one opposable digit that could be considered a thumb. The digits wrapped around the coffee mugs like fingers — albeit, very thick, furry fingers with retracted claw tips just showing. They drank by lifting mug to mouth and lapping up the liquid with the tip of the tongue.

Bracken could have watched for hours, or at least until they finished the pot, but he happened to glance at the counter and see Blaise had found the manual and was absorbed in reading. Bracken hurried to intercept him, on the pretense that he needed to reference it. Blaise relinquished the manual, looking thoughtful, but didn't say anything about it.

*

Whether by science, the heat, or just the essence of coffee, something drew customers by the dozens into The Defiant through the afternoon. Some were human; most were feline.

The tigers were haughty, aware of their superiority, but none were as deadly and aggressive as Shaz had been. One tiger even complimented Bracken's coat.

"It's new," Bracken told her, then added casually, "I don't usually wear clothes."

This caused Aja to raise an eyebrow.

"Aside from hats and the occasional vest, tigers don't wear clothes either," purred the friendly feline. She was petite and silvery with wide blue eyes, and she purred constantly. "But I would make an exception for something as adorable as that coat."

"If I find another I'll let you know," Bracken said obligingly, hoping that continued goodwill would help him to avoid another tiger attack. Fortunately, as a Morpha, acting overly polite came easily to him.

"I'd love it if you did."

Bracken guessed by the forward tilt of her ears that she was pleased; her face never changed expression. As she walked away, he turned to Blaise who was weighing beans with a look of intense concentration. "She's happy, right? I didn't insult her tigerness or anything, I hope."

Blaise glanced over his half-spectacles at the petite tiger who was seating herself at a table. "Yes."

"Yes what?"

"Yes she is happy. It's hard to read tigers, I know."

"If you think their faces are hard to decipher, try their

handwriting," Aja put in. She was still looking through the newspaper, though Bracken suspected she was simply turning the pages to pass the time.

"I don't plan on reading any tiger literature in the near future," said Bracken, who was still coming to terms with their walking, talking and wearing hats.

"If you did, I could help you," said Blaise, going back to his measuring. "I invented a way to translate their language. Jaz was very interested in it."

"Not just theirs," said Aja. "Don't be so modest. His invention can translate anything," she told Bracken. "He has long talks with beetles and lizards sometimes when we're on the road."

"I just wanted to see if I could," Blaise muttered, then said to Bracken, "Tigers communicate by subtext. If you could hear all the things they can say with one ear and the tip of their tail, you'd be amazed. And probably live longer too." Their eyes met briefly and he reddened. "That is… in a general sense…"

Conversation stalled, trading places with anxious silence.

Bracken had put the reason for Blaise and Aja's extended visit out of his mind for a little while, but he couldn't forget it completely. Shaz would return and there would be more bloodshed unless something could be worked out. Aja had hurt Shaz's pride with a blast of repellent to the eyes, and Blaise's formula, on which depended the emancipation of humankind in Xio, was still in Shaz's possession. And Shaz was unlikely to chum up and hand it over.

As he took another order from another tiger, Bracken wondered if curling up in a cabinet would save him if it came to more shooting and mauling.

"It's harder than it looks, isn't it?" said a man sitting at the counter, watching Bracken work.

Bracken had been in a hurry and, leaving the grinder running, had poured beans in the hopper without anything beneath the chute to catch the grounds. Now a layer of brown grit coated everything, including himself.

"I don't know how she does it all. Did it all…" Bracken glanced at the man briefly. He didn't remember seeing him come in, although a few humans had ventured into the shop over the course of the afternoon. Bracken wasn't surprised he couldn't remember serving the man; it had been a hectic few hours, and he'd been more concerned about the tigers than the humans.

"Practice, and inherent perfectionism." The man shrugged broad shoulders, fingering the cuffs of his collared red shirt. "The nice thing about such a complex activity as running a café, is most people don't know how it works. They'll believe you're an expert at anything if you use enough jargon."

Bracken mused on this as he brushed piles of coffee grounds onto the floor, where they mixed with the spilled milk that had been tracked all over the workspace. A seed of an idea was germinating when the front doors opened and an ambush of tigers swaggered in, with Shaz in his top hat leading the invasion.

16

CoffeeSpeak

Blaise backed away until he bumped the back counter. Aja reached for her shotgun.

Bracken took a deep breath and pressed shaking hands down on top of the counter to steady himself. "Hello again. Shaz. How… ah… how are you today?" He tried his best to smile politely.

Shaz stopped before Bracken and stared down at him. His whiskers twitched; the rest of his face remained frozen. "Who are you? Not that it matters. Jaz owes me a shipment of explosives and I'm taking this place as collateral until I get it."

"I paid you with this." Aja tapped the shotgun with a gloved finger. "Or did you need more?"

"Try it," Shaz growled, ears flattening. "My associates and I will turn you into tiger meat."

"Don't you mean human meat?" Aja said with a mean grin.

Shaz froze for a moment, thinking this over. "…I mean what I said."

Bracken jumped in before the retort building behind Aja's lips could shoot out and start another massacre. "You can have The Defiant. You can take over right now. Here's the recipe book. You can use a siphon, right?"

Shaz looked at Bracken, then past him into the workspace, scanning the counters and shelves but not settling on any item in particular. "…yes. Obviously I can use one."

"Great. So, I'll get out of your way and—"

"Excuse me," a soft voice nuzzled into the conversation. The silver female tiger was standing at the counter beside Shaz. "Could I have another?" She pushed an empty mug toward Bracken, adding a purred, "Hello, Shaz."

An answering purr erupted in Shaz's chest automatically. "Sheila. It's… good to see you."

Bracken stared. Behind him, Blaise gawked, open-mouthed. Shaz's temper dropped from blazing hot wrath to pleasant golden felicity in Sheila's presence.

Bracken seized the moment, and Sheila's coffee mug. "Sure. How would you like it? Pourover? Press pot? Siphon? Espresso? Cortado? Pourtado?"

"Whatever I had last was good. Do you have any flavors?"

"We have vanilla, caramel, chocolate…" Bracken glanced at Shaz and continued, "…pomegranate, clorentine, cherry, fruit punch, lemonade, peppermint, spearmint, buttermint, melon, walnut, peanut, pistachio, almond, chocolate and… vanilla… bean." Bracken watched Shaz at the edge of his vision. The tiger's eyes seemed to glass over slightly. Bracken hoped it was due to the complexity of the improved syrup list rather than pure twitterpation.

"I'll have vanilla please," purred Sheila.

"Coming up." Bracken turned to Blaise who was doing a fine impression of a lizard hiding under a rock, but without the rock.

Blaise gulped and held out his hand for the cup, but Bracken spun back to Shaz with a new inspiration. He felt under the counter for the coffee manual, pulled it out and opened it to the most incoherent page of instructions he could find. It had drawings, formulas, a messy table of various numbers, and even several equations in the margins. He pushed the manual across the counter. "Here, you'll need to memorize all this. If you need help with the translation let me know. Coffee language can be pretty tricky. It's organic. Always evolving and changing. Next week it'll probably be totally different."

Blinking, Shaz took the notebook. It looked quite small in his paws.

Bracken turned back to Blaise, eyebrows lifted, holding up the cup. Blaise stared blankly for a moment, then the unspoken question registered. He pointed from his waist to the grinder where several small containers of premeasured beans waited. Bracken went over, took one and dumped the beans in the hopper. The grinder obligingly chewed the beans to the consistency of coarse salt. Bracken deposited this into a press pot, filled the pot with water and agitated the slurry with a long spoon while Blaise stood beside him, murmuring instructions from the corner of his mouth.

"I like his coat," said Sheila, resting her elbows on the counter. "So blue."

"Oh, yes," said Shaz. "Me too. Very nice."

"He oozes gentility from every whisker," Bracken muttered to Blaise as they stood shoulder to shoulder facing the press pot.

"Must keep it in special reserve. Only to be used in emergencies, or to court female tigers," Blaise murmured back.

When the brew was ready, Bracken filled the cup and passed it to Sheila, who thanked him and returned to her table.

Bracken returned to Shaz. "Any questions before I get out of your way, Shaz?"

"I don't..." Shaz had prepared for a fight, but not willing surrender. Certainly not the surrender of an entire coffee shop, the running of which he'd just realized he knew nothing about.

His tiger posse shuffled and muttered behind him, beginning to feel disappointed at the lack of violence. Aja set her chin in her hand, also disappointed. Blaise stood in the background, cracking his knuckles nervously.

"The grinder can be tricky, right, Blaise?" Bracken glanced back toward Blaise, then faced Shaz again. "If you turn it too many clicks the gears dislocate and the rotors will freeze up, but as long as you keep the sprockets oiled and the turners tuned and don't use too many beans at one time you won't have any problems."

"Yes…" Shaz began.

"And the espresso machine needs a tune-up," Bracken continued quickly. "It can be dangerous so I suggest doing it after you close. Sometimes the bloom filter clogs the wand and then you have to shut the boiler down until it cools past eighty or it'll explode."

In the corner of his eye, Bracken saw the man in the red shirt chuckling behind his hand.

"Ah…" Shaz began.

"Name's Bracken." Bracken smiled politely.

"Bracken, I own this place now, so you work for me. I have business to take care of elsewhere in town. You stay here and work. Got it?"

Bracken shrugged. "I guess I could stay on."

Shaz spun and pointed to a table by the window. "That's my table. Don't let anyone else sit there. I own this place,"

Shaz said, as if reinforcing the fact to himself.

"Sure. I'll post a sign." Bracken smiled and nodded.

Shaz nodded. His ears wobbled uncertainly, as if a good thing was happening but he wasn't sure how it had come about.

Shaz glanced around the room, his gaze lingering on Sheila, who was ogling Bracken's coat.

Blaise edged forward and tugged on Bracken's sleeve. "The formula. He still has the formula."

"I bet he'd be willing to trade for it," the man in the red shirt murmured, loud enough for them to hear.

Bracken shook his head. "I can't…"

"For the sake of humanity, please!" Blaise hissed.

Shaz's ears swiveled, and he turned to face them.

"I'd like to propose a trade," Bracken said, getting the words out with effort.

Shaz grunted. "Ehm?"

Bracken nodded toward Sheila. "Your, er, lady friend wants a jacket like mine. I could donate to your cause. You trade me for that recipe you're holding onto — it's still yours after all — and everyone gets what they want."

Shaz mulled on this a while, absently touching the folded slip of paper in his hat band with one claw, letting the idea saturate his mind.

"It's a good deal," Bracken encouraged, his throat somewhat tight. "You give her what she wants, she'll be yours for life."

Shaz's tail and ears went up, and he nodded. Bracken slipped off the coat with a faint sigh and handed it over. Shaz pushed the scrap of paper across the counter to Bracken, and went to Sheila's table with his offering.

Bracken passed the paper to Blaise, who scanned the rumpled surface and looked back at Bracken, beaming like a lizard who owned the biggest rock in the desert. "This is it! Do you know what this piece of paper will do for us?"

Bracken shrugged, smiling faintly.

Blaise interpreted the gesture as modesty. "You've done a great thing, kid. Jaz would be proud of you."

The praise was diminished in the wake of losing his aunt's coat. Even though Blaise approved of his sacrifice, and Jaz would have approved of his completing her mission, Bracken had lost something of Sadie he couldn't recover.

Blaise patted his shoulder. "Hey, don't worry. We'll come back tomorrow and help out."

"Thought we were getting out of town tonight," said Aja. "Have to get back and water those petri dishes."

"I have the formula. Home can wait a day or two," Blaise reasoned, glancing briefly at the coffee manual. "At least we can help the kid find his feet."

"I don't think I'll be here tomorrow," Bracken said. "I just told Shaz I'd stay to keep him pacified for now."

"Guess I don't blame you," Blaise said. "It's a shame

though. People rely on this place. It's a safe haven. With Shaz running things, us humans will likely have to find another place to relax and catch our breath."

"Sorry," said Bracken. "I'd stay if I could but I don't really know anything about this place. I don't belong here."

"Where do you belong?"

The question caught Bracken off guard. "C— ah, I mean…"

Blaise watched him, unblinking.

Bracken stammered for what felt like minutes, but could think of nothing to say. His mind simply shut down. Dealing with tigers and death and more tigers had taken all of Bracken's mental resources. He shrugged, apologetic, then sagged back against the counter, shaking his head. "I… I just mean… I… don't… It's complicated…"

"Give the kid a break, Blaise. He's tuckered, and I'm famished." Aja dismounted her stool and picked up her shotgun, holding it barrel down at her side. "Let's get some lunch."

"But… just one second—"

"No more seconds. Tigers are gone, you got what you wanted. The only threat here is me, if I don't get some food in me right quick."

"Fine… " Blaise sighed. "We'll be back tomorrow, Bracken."

"All right. Um. Thanks for your help."

"Don't mention it." Aja touched the brim of her hat with a gloved finger and strode to the front doors.

Blaise lingered a moment, then followed her. At the doors he turned back suddenly and held up the paper. "And thanks for this! Are you sure we can't repay you? Jaz was interested in my translator..."

Bracken shook his head. "I don't need it now."

"Well, alright. Take care," said Blaise.

Bracken waved, waiting until they were gone and away before letting the smile fade. "I think I'll close early tonight."

17

Café Ghost

It wasn't hard to close early. In fact, the shop was empty by early evening. All of the human patrons had left the café by late afternoon, intent on reaching their homes before dark.

After flirting with Sheila for a while, Shaz took his posse to report to his boss Grayson, and the last remaining feline patrons left to find their evening meals — something Bracken didn't dwell on as he locked the doors and flipped the hanging sign in the window beside them to 'closed.'

Walking with rare purpose and determination, he crossed the café and went downstairs into Sadie's room. Jaz's body was still there on the cot, covered by the blanket, which was now spotted with blood. Bracken swallowed hard and looked away from her. He conducted a thorough search of the room, seeking clues to Sadie's whereabouts. He searched underneath the cot, rummaged through dresser drawers, desk drawers, and even searched in the pockets of clothes on the rack. He found interesting trinkets, pens, bottles of colored ink, blank paper, and rolls of undeveloped film, but nothing to indicate where Sadie had gone after leaving The Defiant. He had thought for sure there would be an address, or name of a hotel in Homburg, or one of the nearby cities. But there was no such thing.

He moved on to Jaz's room. He flipped through each of the daily binders on her desk, proceeding from Monday to Sunday. There were faces, names, newspaper clippings, calendars, columns of dates with short notations about important events in each binder — about five years' worth of dates. Sadie wasn't mentioned in any of them. Bracken dropped the last binder on the floor, letting it fall as it would on top of the others, and then searched the desk drawers.

Nothing.

In the dresser, nothing.

Nothing of interest in the closet.

Nothing beneath the rug.

Aside from the bedroom where he'd found Sadie's jacket, the papers with the sketches and scraps of her stories, and the notations in the coffee manual that he was pretty sure were in her handwriting, there was no physical evidence she had ever been in The Defiant, much less where she had gone from there. But she *had* traveled in The Defiant. Jaz *must* have known where Sadie had gone.

After hours of searching, Bracken found himself standing in the doorway to his — Sadie's — room, staring at Jaz's body, resisting the pointless urge to shake her.

His father's arguments with Sadie rose up in his mind. The voice filled his head, as if his father were speaking right beside him.

Why do you always run away? Your family is here, right here! Do we mean that little to you?

Bracken put his hands over his ears to shut out the echo of the memory and hurried upstairs, into the now darkened shop. Night had fallen while he had been in the basement. He turned on the overhead lights and searched the workspace. Maybe there was some clue to be found beneath the piles of paper and receipts beneath the register—

No.

Maybe on another shelf, behind the syrup bottles and condiments—

No.

Nothing. There was nothing. Sadie had just vanished.

Like she always does, said a small voice in the back of his mind.

"No! I can find her! I *will* find her!" Bracken shouted at the empty shop.

"Perhaps I can help?" a sudden voice spoke behind him.

Bracken jumped and spun to face the man in the red shirt.

The man raised his hands in a non-threatening gesture. "I'm sorry to startle you—"

"Th… the shop's closed," Bracken stammered, glancing at the doors to ensure he had indeed locked them.

"Yes, I know. I was sitting right there at the bar when you locked the doors."

"But the—"

"Shop was empty. I know." The man dropped his hands to his sides. "It happens a lot. People don't usually notice me unless I want them to. Or unless they're a passenger in The Defiant, of course, or have traveled in it before."

Bracken backed further into the workspace as the man stepped toward him. "Who are you?"

"My name is Janus." He pronounced it 'Yanus.' "I am also trapped here. I have been here nearly as long as Jaz, in fact."

"She never mentioned you."

"There's a lot she doesn't mention."

Bracken had to agree with this. He studied the man, recognizing the gray-streaked black hair, the square shoulders, and spotless red collared shirt. One thing he hadn't noticed before was the man's eyes. They were quite… odd.

"You have seen me before," Janus confirmed, nodding. "You just didn't *notice*."

He walked to the pourover station, stepping over syrup bottles and boxes of condiments Bracken had left on the floor during his frantic search. Brushing aside loose stacks of napkins, he began making himself coffee. He picked up a tin full of pre-ground coffee that Bracken had prepared earlier in the day and forgotten about, frowned slightly and opened a bag of whole beans.

Bracken swallowed. "You were here when… Jaz… died?"

Janus measured and ground the beans before answering. "I was here. There was nothing I could have done, any more than you could have if you'd tried." He glanced over at Bracken when he said this. The man's eyes were gray in color, textured like cut stone, rather than smooth and glasslike. But that wasn't the really strange thing about them. His cornea and pupils were square. In fact, they were a series of squares, which grew smaller and smaller toward the center, like a tunnel. They made Bracken feel off balance. He looked away. When he looked at Janus again, the man was taking a steaming kettle from a heating element.

"So, you're looking for Sadie," Janus mused, watching water stream from the kettle's spout to the bed of coffee grounds in the vessel. When viewed from the side, his eyes were even more disconcerting. They were concave in the center. Instead of rounding outward like a normal human eye, they dipped inward. Bracken wondered if they were *actual* tunnels, going into the depths of the man's head. The thought made Bracken's skin prickle.

"She's my aunt." Bracken couldn't look at the man's eyes

anymore. He fixed his gaze on Janus's chin instead.

"I know. She talked about you often."

"You knew her?"

"Quite well. She lived with us for many years."

"Do you know where she is now?"

Janus set the kettle down. "Not exactly. But that's not the question you should be asking. What you should be asking is why."

Bracken blinked. "Why?"

"Why did Sadie leave The Defiant. Why *would* she leave it? If you can answer that question, you'll probably find the answer to the other."

Bracken clenched the edge of the counter with both hands. "Please, if you know something, tell me."

Janus tossed the filter and spent grounds in the waste bin and poured coffee into a cracked mug. "I can help you find your aunt, if you'll help me with something."

"What?" Bracken watched Janus sip from the mug, and realized after a moment that it was the same one Jaz had been drinking from that morning.

Janus leaned against the counter facing him. "I want what Jaz wants."

"Wanted…"

"I want freedom. Help me get that and I will help you find the answer to your question."

"How do I do that?"

"Start by translating the Sassacus book in Jaz's room. The book will tell you what you need to know. It would have been good if you'd traded Blaise his formula for the translator, but you can try again next week. And also, staying alive would help." He took a sip of coffee. "Speaking of which, you ought to study that coffee manual. It's a trove of information."

Bracken hurried around the counter and retrieved the manual, shaking a layer of coffee grounds off of the cover. He was returning to his seat when the shop reset.

Chairs banged upside-down onto tables. Items jumped from the floor where Bracken had left them, back to their proper places. Only a few things, like Wednesday's binder and the forgotten tin of coffee grounds, remained where they were. The bucket reappeared under the faucet, which was suddenly running again, and the dishwasher door fell open, emitting a cloud of steam. The countertops smoothed themselves, the gouges left by Shaz's claws vanishing.

"Everything returns to its original position at midnight," Janus was sitting at the counter, cracked mug in hand. Bracken didn't remember seeing him move to a stool. He was just… there.

Bracken shut off the faucet and then joined Janus at the counter. Bracken opened the manual and found a list of coffees, written in the sophisticated, loopy handwriting:

DEFIANT COFFEES

*Cinnamon Toast – Cinnamon, vanilla,
butter, honey (light roast)*

*Eden (blueberry roast) – blueberry,
floral, almond (light roast)*

*Sugar 'n' Spice – cloves, pastry,
baked apple (light roast)*

*Breakfast Blend – maple, roasted hazelnut,
cherry (medium, but call it dark*)*

Black Ivory – citrus, walnut, tobacco (medium)

**Most people, when requesting a dark roast, really
mean 'something that does not taste of dirt or
cardboard but with a strong burst of smokiness akin
to the taste of a charred log'. That, to them, means
properly roasted beans. Jaz holds no such belief.
She says she roasts for flavor, not for showcasing
her ability to produce oily bits of charcoal.*

But for customers expecting the 'dark' element, we have the benignly named Breakfast Blend, which has that coveted charcoal note, but stops short of obliterating the equally valid notes of caramelized sugar, toasted hazelnut and cherry the beans have to offer. More discerning drinkers describe the taste of Jaz's Breakfast Blend as 'cherry preserves and maple spread over burnt toast.' Everyone else describes it as 'pretty good.'

Bracken felt sure he wouldn't like whoever had written this. They sounded like one of his teachers back home, who was always trying to make herself seem important.

He turned to another page and found a note written by Sadie which was much more helpful:

- REMEMBER TO SHUT
THE DISHWASHER!

- The paper cups in the cupboard will always fall out when you open the door, no matter how carefully you put them away. Just don't open that cupboard.

- That bottle of vanilla syrup that resets with the shop WILL displace anything you put in its spot, even cash or napkins, or another syrup bottle — which will explode if it's displaced, and will cover the whole workspace in stickiness. You've been warned.

- There is a vanilla glitch in The Defiant. Every customer, from any world, will always order vanilla. We don't know why. I've even asked Janus about it and he doesn't know. Jaz always gives customers three flavor choices. She says if she doesn't, people get irritated for some reason, and they complain about it and demand she get more flavors, and it's a huge waste of time. They seem to know this is happening, but they want to think they have choices, even if they can't help always getting vanilla anyway.

Bracken was trying to absorb this, rubbing his temples with his fingers, when the basement door banged open and Jaz stomped out.

"What did you do to my room? It looks like a tornado went through it."

Bracken looked up, startled. Then he gaped. Then he tried to stand, got tangled in the barstool and fell over backward.

"Ja — aah!"

Jaz strode into the workspace and stared around her. She frowned and picked up the tin of coffee grounds that Janus had shunned, opened it, and frowned even more. "And what happened to these beans? They're ruined!"

18

Moody Indigo

Jaz inspected the expired grounds, scowling. "I'm gone for one day and you trash the place…"

Bracken crashed around a bit, separating himself from the stool. "Jaz! You died!"

"Only for a day." She dumped the grounds in the garbage, wincing at the loss.

"I saw you die," Bracken insisted pointlessly. "I was there." He hopped over the counter and hugged her.

Jaz slowly raised a hand and patted his shoulder with her fingertips. "It wasn't planned, I admit."

"How?" Bracken pulled away, searching her face.

Jaz shrugged, matter-of-fact. "It's the shop. It brings me back every time."

"Every time? How many times have you died?"

"I lost count." She dislodged herself from his grip and looked away, scanning the workspace and counters. "Hey, were you using my cup?"

"No, it was Janus—" Bracken turned to the counter where Jaz's cracked mug sat. Janus was gone. "Where did he go?"

Jaz's mouth tightened, and she cast a suspicious glance around the room. "You met Janus?"

Bracken nodded. "He showed up a little while ago."

She spun to face Bracken, grabbing his arm. "What did he say to you? Did he ask you for something?"

"He just said he's trapped like you and wants help getting out."

Jaz stepped over to the counter and picked up the mug. Frowning at the contents, she emptied it in the sink and rinsed it. "Don't talk to him. He's dangerous."

"He didn't seem dangerous." Bracken thought it pretty rude of Jaz to dump out Janus's coffee before he could finish it. But then, it was no more rude than Janus using Jaz's mug knowing she wasn't really dead.

"Take it from me that he is." Jaz shook excess water from the mug and set it on a shelf below the espresso machine. "What else happened while I was gone?"

"I turned the shop over to Shaz to keep him from killing anyone else. And I gave Sadie's coat—"

"Wait, you gave him the shop?"

"Yeah, but it's okay. I told him I'd run things, since he doesn't know anything about making coffee."

Jaz snorted. "Neither do you."

"He didn't know that. Besides, I thought you were dead. You didn't tell me you'd revive at midnight."

"I told you the shop resets. I'm part of the shop. Now I have to deal with Shaz thinking he's the boss here." She scowled, massaging the space between her eyebrows with two fingers.

"I got the formula back," Bracken told her, somewhat curtly.

"You did?" She lowered her hand, relief spreading over her face. "How?"

"Shaz wanted to woo this tiger named Sheila—"

Jaz rolled her eyes. "He's been after her for ages."

"And she wanted a coat like mine, so I traded Shaz for the formula and he gave her the coat."

Jaz grabbed Bracken by the shoulders, eyes shining. "And you traded it to Blaise for the translator? Good boy!"

"…no. I figured I didn't need to, since you were dead."

Jaz's grin dropped. She spun away, punching her fists down at her sides with a groan. "Bracken…"

"You were dead!" He threw out his arms to either side.

Jaz slumped onto the counter, rocking her forehead on her arms and stamping the same foot repeatedly.

"I got Blaise his formula at least! You could be happy about that."

"That doesn't help me," Jaz moaned, voice muffled.

"I lost Sadie's coat too. I guess you don't care about that either."

Jaz sagged and thumped down on the floor. She sat back against the shelves, closing the dishwasher door with a sharp kick. It bounced back down. She kicked it again. "I don't care about your frothing coat. It's just a coat."

Bracken glared. "It was Sadie's!"

"Then you should have been more careful with it." The dishwasher door fell open again. Jaz jumped up, slamming it closed with her palm. "Hell's *rotting* eyes!" She grabbed the full bucket in the sink and heaved, launching it over the tea counter. White rags and foaming water cascaded over the tins, surging across the counter and splashing on the floor. The bucket bounced, somersaulting, flinging more water across tables and chairs before dropping and rolling on the floor.

Bracken flinched and stepped back.

"Wand sucking—"Jaz kicked at the spreading puddle at her feet, slipped and fell heavily on her side. She got to her feet, lurching to the tea counter. Grabbing tea tins with both hands, she pitched them at the windows, along with more profanity. The panes pinged with each hit, and the dented tins clattered across the floor, bumping the bucket and the legs of tables and chairs. The noise was awful.

When her arsenal was gone, Jaz slammed her fists on the countertop, bunching her shoulders, breathing heavily through her nose. "I'm sorry," she said.

Bracken watched her, saying nothing.

"I'd gotten my hopes up. That book is the closest I've come to finding a way out of here since… since a long time."

"I get it," Bracken said softly.

"No, Bracken. You don't get it."

"We can still get the translator. Blaise said he'd be back tom— next week."

"Next week is too late. I have to return the book today."

Bracken hesitated, wondering if he should mention the idea just occurring to him; if he should raise her hopes again. But regardless of what he didn't understand, he knew that Jaz needed a win, and he owed her all the help he could give. "It's not too late if we have pictures of the pages to translate later. We can photograph them with my camera. Then we just have to get the pictures developed and you'll have them for as long as you need."

Jaz turned as this registered, a small hope lighting her eyes. "It's a big book. But, if we start now, we might have it all done before Huey gets here in…" She looked toward the clock. "…six or seven hours."

"Who's Huey?"

"He borrowed the book for me."

Bracken smirked, lifting an eyebrow. "Borrowed, with permission?"

"Sort of…" Jaz didn't meet his eyes.

His jaw dropped. "You stole it? Ha!"

"I didn't steal it."

"Right. You got this Huey guy to steal it for you."

"No… are you even listening? He borrowed it first, then gave it to me to keep overnight—"

"So for a week."

"Yeah but he doesn't know about all that. All he knows is he owes me for letting him run his betting operations here."

 Bracken gave a low whistle. "Wow, Jaz."

"Wow what?"

"You smuggle slugs, you trade explosives, fight tigers, host betting operations. You're a crime master."

"Thanks," she said flatly, then glanced at the clock above the doors. "You better start photographing. It's going to take a while."

"But I want to hear more about your life of crime." He also wanted to know more about Janus, what he was and how he'd gotten trapped, but that could wait.

"After we get the book copied." She pushed him toward the basement door.

"Why didn't you just borrow the book yourself?" Bracken asked over his shoulder.

"Just go. I'll tell you all about it another time."

19

Scribbles

Several hours later, Bracken bent over the open book on the cleared desk in Jaz's office, squinting through the camera viewfinder at another page of scribbles. He'd photographed about a hundred pages and had over half the book remaining. The Sassacus script, which was scribbly to begin with, seemed to congeal into mats of black ink. Now and then a stroke of red dashed across certain parts, but that barely relieved the monotony.

The tome's pages looked just like those in notebooks he and his younger sister had blackened testing a pen Sadie had brought one year. She claimed it had everlasting ink. They had filled ten notebooks, then proceeded through newspapers, receipts and even napkins. They had scrawled for hours, until their fingers were black and their hands were cramped, but that effort was nothing compared to the work of these Sassacus scribble masters.

Bracken had just photographed a page so black it could have been used as a paint chip, and was framing a page with a dash of red running along the bottom edge, when Jaz came in and stood behind him with an open box of cherry cobbler, looking over his shoulder.

"How's it coming?" she asked.

"You're in my light."

"Sorry." She sidestepped.

"Still in my light."

She sat on the edge of the bed and placed her feet between two stacks of binders he'd moved to make room on the desk. She balanced the pastry box on her knees and forked up a bite. "So how's it coming?"

Bracken returned to his task. "Almost done."

She beamed. "Really?"

"No." The shutter clicked; a page turned. "This book goes on forever."

"Huey will be here at noon," Jaz reminded Bracken, stirring the cobbler with her fork.

"Huey will have to wait until I'm done. Are you sure this is a language?"

"Yes. You can't go any faster?"

Bracken shot her a narrow look over his shoulder. "If you want, you can take over here and I'll go make the coffee."

She stood. "I'll get out of your hair then."

"Do." Bracken didn't mean to be curt, but his back felt like ten spikes had been driven into it and the book seemed to be getting longer the more pages he turned. He wanted to help Jaz, but he hadn't expect helping to be so painful.

Jaz paused at the door. "Want anything from upstairs?"

"A massage and a tuna salad."

"How about cobbler and coffee?"

"Fine…" He hunched over the tome again as she went out.

Less than two minutes later, she swept back in with a coffee mug and the box of cobbler. "Bracken! Bracken, this is bad. Oz is here." She dropped the box onto the bed with a thump.

Bracken straightened, knuckling the small of his back. "Who?"

She gestured with the mug, sloshing liquid onto the rug. "Oz! The courier who handles the books. Huey told him to pick up the book *here* for some reason — I knew he'd mess this up!"

Bracken took the mug from her before she dropped it. "I thought you were giving the book to Huey."

"But *he* got it from Oz!"

"Okay?" Bracken sipped and blinked, looking at the cup. He'd expected coffee, or even tea, but found it was only water.

Jaz must have been distracted indeed.

"Oz doesn't know I have it!" Jaz clenched her head with both hands. "Rotting son of a—"

Bracken set the cup on the desk beside the tome. "Jaz, please. You're hurting my ears. Can you just tell me what is going on? And this time try not to leave stuff out."

"The lady who owns the book won't let me borrow from her after I lost one of her other books in Langston, all right? There was a fire…" Jaz's eyes drifted to one side and her tone became vague. "Or a holocaust? It got burned. That's all I remember. So I got blacklisted from borrowing any more books." Jaz looked back at him. "Huey's brother Tago has borrowing privileges from the Sassacus library—"

Bracken coughed. "There are more of these?"

"I just said there's a library."

"Of scribble books? That's ridiculous."

"It's not scribble, it's Sassacus. Now listen. Huey borrowed this book under his brother's name. His brother owns a casino in Alchaven and is very connected. The owner of the library lends by courier—"

"This Oz guy."

"And he's here right now. If he finds out Huey loaned me the book, he'll take it away immediately, Huey's brother will get blacklisted, and I'll never get another chance at this book or any other, and I'll never find the white-haired man!"

Bracken squinted at her, trying to remember details. "And the white-haired man is…"

"The guy who trapped me here!" Jaz grabbed Bracken's shoulders. "We can't let Oz know I have the book!"

"Ow, Jaz. Careful of the camera." Bracken shrugged her off. "He doesn't know you have it yet, does he?"

Jaz backed away and prowled the room anxiously. "No, but he suspects something is up."

Bracken rubbed his eyes, trying to think. At the same time he wondered how *he* became the adult in this situation. But then, if Jaz was frantic, the situation was probably pretty serious — at least, to her. "Okay. Why don't you just… go make the coffee and act natural. I'll bring the book up when I'm done. I'll hide it in a pastry box or something. When Huey gets here, you can give him the box and pretend there's pastry inside. Then he can slip it out and give it to Oz later."

"You can copy the rest of the book, right? Do you have enough film?" Jaz rubbed her hands together, then cracked her knuckles one by one.

Bracken winced at the sound and turned back to the book. "Yes, it's fine. Just go and handle things until I come up."

He waited until the door closed, and set the camera down, groping a distraught hand through his hair. He didn't know if he would ever finish the job, at the rate it was proceeding. He just couldn't say so to Jaz though. It was his fault she couldn't translate the book and get the information she needed to escape The Defiant. He'd have to go as fast as he could and hope Jaz kept things under control upstairs until he finished. That desperate, pleading look she'd been giving him was unnerving.

Returning to the desk, he turned the page of the tome with more force than necessary, and his hand hit the mug he'd set nearby. It shot off the desk and landed on the pile of binders on the floor, splashing water all over them. Bracken hissed angrily and grabbed the stack up out of the spreading puddle. It was a good effort, but the stack wobbled and pitched forward, spilling loose pages, pictures and paper scraps across the rug. He hastily shoved the papers and photographs into piles, away from the spill. He could sort them later; for now they just needed to stay dry and out of the way until he finished his task.

He snatched up several photographs which had escaped a fat envelope containing more of the same. One of the photos caught his eye and he paused, looking closer at it. Then he turned to the desk and turned back several pages in the tome. He stopped at one page that had a memorable red stroke resembling a half-butterfly, left center of the page, and he held the photo up beside it.

They were the same.

Bracken felt as if the floor had suddenly dropped away.

He pulled out several more photos, and these matched more pages in the book. The last photo he picked up was of a book's cover. He compared it to the front of the tome and saw that they too were the same.

Bracken sank onto the bed, the packet of photos clutched between his knees. He stayed there, eyes bulging, rocking slightly, for several minutes. Then he searched for every escaped picture of scribble writing and returned them to the envelope. He went into his room and slipped the envelope into his backpack, then returned to Jaz's room and picked up the box of cobbler she had left on the bed. He dumped the contents into a small wastebasket, lined the bottom of the box with dry paper scavenged from the desk and put the tome inside the box.

After taking several deep breaths to calm himself — which only made him feel lightheaded — he carried the heavy package up the stairs and entered the café.

20

Ambiguousness

Jaz took an empty teapot from a patron's table, adding it to the growing collection on her tray. The patron — an elf — murmured thanks, stood smoothly and glided toward the doors in a whisper of silks. She watched them join the procession of similarly dressed pedestrians who moved along the sidewalk in groups of twos and threes, talking quietly among themselves. A light breeze stirred the feathery leaves of trees lining the road, causing a languid shower of pink petals that brushed the windows of The Defiant as they fell.

Thursday was Elf Day, when The Defiant stood on a quiet street in Houzai, a country famous for its advanced technology, relatively peaceful nature, and its inhabitants being the most beautiful and intelligent of all races in the world. Jaz had mixed feelings about Elf Day. It was generally quiet, with little chance of getting mauled to death or extorted, but on the other hand, she found elves to be rigid and fussy. Not to mention, they preferred tea over coffee, so Jaz would spend the day collecting used teapots and washing them, to be immediately used again.

It took more effort than tea should, in Jaz's opinion. Tea in general was fine. She liked it. What annoyed her was how elves managed to make even the simple process of soaking leaves in hot water complicated.

Jaz stood beside the table, staring at the windows and following this line of thought for as long as possible. This allowed her to ignore the presence of the courier, Oz, who sat at the counter, watching her with quiet green eyes. Oz was Cialos, a race rarely seen outside of their far-off native country, whose bodies were almost entirely composed of water. Like the elves, Cialos were beautiful, graceful, with flawless skin and silky hair, but unlike elves, their skin was smooth, no wrinkles or folds, even at the knuckles or eyes, where skin would naturally crease. Neither did they have fingernails, eyebrows or eyelashes, unless they chose to form those details upon themselves, which they rarely did.

Like Morphas, Cialos could change shape. Unlike Morphas, who changed color and form, Cialos took a more random approach; transforming fingers into spikes, arms into whips, toes into sawblades; manipulating their mass to be pliable and smooth as seaweed or armorlike and abrasive as coral; taking on these attributes without warning or intent, unaware of — or indifferent to — injury caused to whoever or whatever was near them when they did.

Oz was one of the few Cialos who had left his homeland and the only one Jaz had met who wore clothing and had a job. The choice seemed to have been made on a whim, though his worshipful devotion to his employer, who among other things curated a large collection of ancient texts, probably factored into it.

More customers entered, forcing her to return to the register, and then to the tea counter to prepare yet another pot of tea.

"You seem agitated, Jaz. Were you surprised to see me?" Oz sipped water from a pint glass. He wore a yellow and black checkered vest. A matching motorcycle helmet sat on the counter near him.

"I thought I was on your list of people to shun," Jaz said casually, keeping her eyes on her work.

"You are." Oz adjusted the leather strap of the carrier's satchel across his chest. "But I'm supposed to meet someone here. He's returning an item."

"Ah."

"You probably know him." Oz set down the glass and rested smooth, milky hands on the counter, one atop the other. "It's Huey Castelaine."

Jaz took the teapot and two mugs to the waiting customers, then without waiting for Oz to say more when she returned to the workspace, took a trayful of dirty teapots the sink to load them in the dishwasher. She took her time, hoping when she finished Bracken would be there, or Oz wouldn't be, but Oz remained at the counter when she had dried the last pot, and Bracken had not appeared.

"Hubert Castelaine borrows a book from my patron," Oz said in near-monotone, sounding bored, but still watching her, "and then arranges to meet me here to return it, instead of at the tea shop which is closer to the port and more convenient for him. Why, I wonder."

Jaz couldn't tell if Oz was being sarcastic or introspective. It was hard to tell anything about his kind: everything about them was ambiguous, from their tones and expressions to their gender. Sadie had less trouble reading Oz than Jaz; they had even seemed to have a rapport until the unfortunate book-burning episode; but Sadie was gone. Jaz half suspected that was the real reason Oz hadn't visited The Defiant in so long.

"He likes my coffee," said Jaz, watching tea leaves expand in the pot. "And I don't ship to Alchaven; too much stuff gets hijacked there. He'd have been coming to Houzai anyway to meet you. He probably wanted to avoid an extra stop."

"Elves don't drink coffee."

"He's half human. Maybe he puts it in his tea." Jaz took the teapot and two cups to the waiting customers.

When she came back, Oz propped his head on a raised fist, looking past her toward the basement door. "And who's this, now?"

Bracken had just emerged, shutting the door behind him. He held a pastry box in one hand and rubbed his chin absently.

Jaz moved toward him, eyebrows raised and hopeful. He seemed distracted, staring at her but not seeing her. "This is Bracken." She laid a hand on his arm. "Bracken, this is Oz."

"And who is he?" Oz persisted.

Bracken blinked, refocusing, and leaned around Jaz to see Oz. "I'm the hired help. Hi."

Oz's eyes flitted to Bracken, then back to Jaz. "He's not as pretty as the last one you had. Where did you find him?"

"He found me." Jaz squeezed Bracken's arm and inclined her head interrogatively. He bobbed the pastry box slightly in response.

"Mhm. What is in the box?" Oz asked Bracken.

"Huh?"

Oz inclined his head toward the pastry box as Jaz had done.

"Just cobbler. I was about to tell Jaz it's... bad." Bracken tipped his hand and let the box slide heavily into the trash can.

Jaz hiccupped, swallowing a rising exclamation.

21

Café Farce

The front doors opened then, admitting Huey Castelaine. He was slender but muscled, his shoulders wide and his waist trim. His ears were longer than a human's but shorter than an elf's, tapered like teardrops and set off by wavy, honey-colored hair. His blue eyes were large and friendly. His mouth was set in a grin balanced pleasingly between a triangle and half-moon. He wore a white suit coat, a maroon vest and pinstriped pants, all perfectly fitted. Some white dust clung to his black leather shoes and the cuffs of his pants.

"Heya, Jaz," he called. Then, seeing who sat at the counter, "Hey… Oz. You're… here." His grin widened and kept widening to the full width of his face.

Jaz's neck muscles ached with the strain of not turning to look in the trash can.

"I hope that's not a problem for you," Oz said.

"A problem? No, of course not." Huey strode to the counter and settled on a stool beside Oz. "I was early myself, as you see. I needed to get some… coffee and stuff here anyway, so…"

"I wasn't aware you drank coffee," said Oz.

"Coffee, tea, wine, beer — you name it." Huey's grin was plastic. "I love Jaz's… dark roast."

"Which one?"

"Jaz, what's that dark roast I love called again?"

"That would be Sugar 'n' Spice," said Jaz.

Huey's eyebrows twitched. "Really? That's what it's called."

"Same thing it was called last time you had it." Her previous encounters with Huey, who spent most of his time in casinos in the lawless country of Alchaven, had given Jaz had the impression that in the event of some horrible disaster or life-threatening situation, Huey could shake off his flippancy which often made him seem ridiculous, and perform intelligently — even bravely — but that event had not yet happened. At least, not in her store.

Bracken suddenly walked toward the counter opposite where Oz sat. "The other assistant you mentioned. Was it a girl named Sadie?"

Shielded from Oz's view for the moment, Jaz sidled against the trash can and, keeping her eyes in his direction, reached inside for the pastry box that held the book.

"Yes," Oz said. "She was also Apeili."

"Apeili?" asked Bracken.

"A shapechanger, of course. Like you."

"You can tell I'm…"

"Of course."

Huey leaned to one side, catching Jaz's attention and waggling his eyebrows as if to ask, 'What's going on? Why is he here?'

Jaz widened her eyes as if to respond, 'I don't know, he just showed up.'

Huey widened his eyes and tilted his head a fraction, wondering, 'where the devil is the book now, and has Oz seen it?'

Jaz shook her head no. Her hand tapped the rim of the trash can.

Huey's mouth dropped open as if an unpleasant taste had just entered it.

Oz leaned to one side, looking past Bracken at Jaz. "The other one was Apeili too, isn't that right?"

Jaz's fingers spasmed on the edge of the can, crackling the plastic liner. "Huh?"

"Your last employee was Apeili."

"Yeah."

Huey joined Oz at the counter, lounging far over it on his elbow, drawing Oz's gaze to him as he asked Bracken, "You're Apeili, eh? Been away from the homeland long?"

"Not very long," said Bracken.

"Ah. That explains it," Huey said with a jerky nod.

With one eye on Oz, Jaz quickly reached into the trash can, lifting out the pastry box.

"What explains what?" Bracken asked.

"Why you're still sane," said Oz. "Apeili who leave their homeland don't adjust well to different cultures."

"Neither do Cialos," Huey said.

"We're quite insane from the start," Oz told him.

There was no way to tell if Oz was serious or not, so Bracken simply asked, "How many ah… races are there, exactly?"

"Eight," said Oz.

Huey listed them helpfully. "Elven, human, Seidyrian, Cialos, Apeili, Kyra Kyth, Sassacus and Nykul."

"And some scattered halfbreeds," said Oz. "Here in Houzai you'll mostly see humans and elves."

"Jaz is a halfbreed, aren't you, Jaz?" said Huey, and nodded to Bracken. "You can tell by the hair."

"Uh huh." She wasn't. "Come and get your coffee."

Huey hurried to meet Jaz at the gap between the tea counter and the wall. She had gone into the kitchen and returned carrying a large, brown paper bag of coffee beans. She thumped it down on the counter and they leaned over it, giving it a close inspection.

"Jaz," Huey said through his teeth, pretending to read the tasting notes scrawled on the front, "I need that… item."

"What were you bloody thinking, meeting him here?" Her whisper was a shout that lacked volume.

Huey winced. "I thought I could get it before he came."

"You are *killing* me." Jaz shoved the bag against his chest and wheeled away. Huey clutched it with one arm and grinned nervously at the room.

Jaz came back with a second bag of beans and dropped it next to the first. "You are buying these," she whispered fiercely.

"Fine, fine, but where is…"

Jaz went to the back counter and brushed wet coffee grounds off the pastry box, carrying it nonchalantly to Huey. She set it down with an air of triumph.

He peeked under the lid. "This is… half a blueberry cobbler."

Jaz snapped her jaws shut and returned, white-faced, to the trash can. With her back to Bracken and Oz, she arbitrarily pulled napkins out of a dispenser with one hand while fishing inside the can with the other until she found the correct box.

Huey took it and, after raising the lid, smiled at Jaz with relief. "My favorite."

They turned back to Oz who was saying to Bracken, "I suppose you're looking for the doorway generator too."

Bracken blinked. "The what?"

"Like the one before you. She asked me about it numerous times." He looked to Huey who, having dumped the book from the box into his satchel, had just closed the top.

"I'll take the book now, if you're done making your purchase."

"Huh? Oh, yeah," said Huey, shuffling toward Oz with the bag pinched between his fingers. "Got it right here."

He had only taken a few steps when Oz extended a hand toward him. His fingers stretched past Bracken and several empty stools along the counter to the satchel. One finger slashed a long hole down one side of it, and the others slipped inside and pulled out the tome, wrapped around it like thin white ribbons. They retracted back into his hand and he put the tome carefully into his satchel without expression.

Huey stood quite still, clutching his own torn satchel, watching Oz's hands until they returned to normal. When they did, he glanced at Jaz and let out a soft sigh. She relaxed against the counter with a similar sigh.

"What's a doorway generator?" Bracken asked.

"It was created by Janus, master of doorways. Some legends say he had two faces, so he could stand on the threshold and look simultaneously into two worlds," said Oz. "Or into time, depending on the legend."

"Janus?" Bracken looked over his shoulder at Jaz.

She kept her face vague and shrugged.

"Yes, Janus. A Lumenatra. Beings from outside our dimension, with immense power, capable of massive destruction," Oz said. "Though many believe the Lumenatra are only a myth…"

"Sadie was looking for something Janus made? Why?" asked Bracken.

"She never told me. She was quite adamant about finding it though," said Oz. "We corresponded for a time."

Jaz jolted at this. "You did?"

Bracken's voice rose slightly and he leaned toward Oz, gripping the edge of the counter. "Did she go into y—somewhere in Houzai? Is that where she is now?"

Jaz froze, a slow horror coming over her as the conversation veered in a direction she'd avoided since Bracken had begun traveling with her. Because she still could not bring herself to say what Oz was so casually saying now.

"No. She's dead."

22

Portrait of Sadie

For the second time that day, Bracken felt as if the floor dropped out from under him. He blinked at Oz, then looked at Jaz. "No… no, she's not. I mean, she's… just… But she's not dead. Right, Jaz?"

Oz also looked at Jaz. "I assumed that was the case when she stopped sending correspondences. Sadie was quite dogged in her search for the doorway generator, so much that only two things could explain her sudden silence. Either she had found the generator, or she had died trying."

"No, no. You're thinking of someone else. Right, Jaz? He means someone else." Bracken drummed his fingers on the counter, trying to hide their sudden shaking.

"You probably don't even remember everyone who's… worked with you, over the years, do you, Jaz?"

Jaz raised a hand to her forehead, half covering her eyes.

Huey shuffled his feet in the uncomfortable silence, smiling again, his eyes flicking nervously from face to face. "Ah, I've got what I came for and gave what I came to give, so I guess I'll say goodbye."

When no one responded, Huey edged to the doors and slid out, clutching his bags of coffee beans

Bracken couldn't stop watching Jaz. Why wasn't she answering him?

"I suppose I'll go too," said Oz. He stood and shouldered his satchel. "If you do happen to find the generator, please let me know."

Jaz lowered her hand from her eyes. "Huh?"

"The doorway generator. If you are still looking for it," Oz said. "My employer has taken an interest in the device. If it can be found, she would pay well for a chance to see it."

Jaz took an unsteady breath. "That was Sadie's project. I wasn't in on it much. I don't think it actually exists."

"Doesn't it? Hm." Oz started for the doors. "Goodbye then. Give my regards to Athamas."

Bracken blinked, finally breaking his stare to glance at Oz. "Who's Athamas?"

"You haven't met him?" asked Oz, an expression approaching surprise crossing his pale face.

Bracken shook his head. "Not yet."

"You're in for a treat then. Goodbye." Oz left them in their disquiet, slipping outside where he mounted his scooter and motored away.

Bracken waited until the doors closed. Then he was moving, striding over to Jaz, grabbing her by the shoulders and looking into her face. "Where's Sadie?"

"…she passed away. About five years ago… six months by your time, I think." Jaz's voice grew hoarse. "I'm sorry."

Bracken gripped her shoulders harder. "Are you serious? Are. You. Serious?"

Jaz nodded, eyes fixed on the ground.

"Jaz! Why didn't you tell me?" He heard his voice echo in the room. Was he shouting? He could barely hear himself past the static filling his head.

She's not dead. She's dead. It's too late. She's not *dead! No! No, no, nonononono…*

But it made sense too. The way her room seemed to have been lived in, her clothes still on the hangers. The unfinished projects on her desk. As if she had been there one day and then… not there the next.

Jaz's eyes came up to meet his. They were reddened, filled with tears. "I couldn't, remember?"

"That was before! You could have told me anytime once I got stuck here, but you let me think…" Bracken's voice cracked, and he had to stop and swallow hard.

Jaz didn't meet his eyes. Her voice was hoarse, just above a whisper. "I can't talk about this right now."

"What is wrong with you? She's my aunt! I deserve to know! So does my family." Bracken pointed a shaking finger at her. "You knew where we lived, because every time she visited she came back here and I'm sure she told you all about us. Why didn't you reach out to us?"

Jaz swiped the back of her hand across her cheekbones. She still refused to look at him, which made Bracken even angrier.

"My family thinks she's still alive somewhere!" Even though they would have been more relieved than saddened to hear that Sadie was gone for good, they still deserved to know."

"What would I have said? I wouldn't be able to tell your family anything besides she's dead. I couldn't even explain how or when."

"How did she die? At least tell me that. Was she killed?"

"No. It wasn't like that. She just… got old."

"She wasn't old," Bracken protested. "She wasn't even thirty the last time she visited."

"But time passes differently here. Remember? A week out there is seven weeks in here. One year is seven. Sadie wasn't the only person who's traveled with me. But she did stay the longest." Jaz's eyes drifted downward, seeing memories of days past. "She traveled with me for almost fifty years."

Bracken's mouth dropped open. "Fifty?"

Jaz nodded. "The Defiant has… an effect on those who travel in it. Not as drastic as what happens with me, but… some things are affected when the shop resets. Wounds heal, for one thing. And the body… doesn't age. We thought that since she didn't look older, she actually wasn't aging, like I don't age. But we were wrong. I don't have a set lifespan. But she did."

"But… but… that would mean…"

Jaz looked in pain, her mouth and eyes tight. "She was over seventy years old when she passed on."

"Seventy…" Bracken mouthed the word, staring at her, still gripping her shoulders.

Jaz didn't try to shrug him off. "I should have told you. I know. You were just so… so set on getting her back, I… I didn't know what… might happen if you found out she was gone."

Bracken just stared at her.

Jaz cleared her throat and pushed on. "And not only that she'd lived here, but what here is, and why she stayed, and what she was doing, and… and everything. It's… it's complicated and—"

Bracken shook his head. "No, it's not. You just didn't want to bother. You were too busy with your big plans for escape—"

Jaz snapped back, quick tears dropping down her cheeks.

"Hey! I care. I'm scared to death you'll get hurt before you can go home. You've seen what can happen here. She'd never forgive me if—"

The doors opened, admitting a new customer, who stared at them in mild surprise. Bracken released Jaz's shoulders and stepped back. Jaz wiped her face with the heels of her hands and moved to the register, leaving Bracken where he stood.

The static filling Bracken's mind grew, filling his vision with red sparks, his body moving automatically to the basement door and down the stairs. He paced outside Sadie's room — old room — clenching and unclenching his fists. Suddenly he spun and punched Jaz's door, leaving a small and unsatisfactory dent in the thick wood. Inspired by Oz's display earlier, he drew back his fist, reshaped it into a thick spike, and punched again. This time, he left a large hole in the wood. His arm throbbed, but he wouldn't feel the full pain until much later. He shook away splinters, drew back and punched again.

Again.

Again.

Now could see into her room through the holes.

Again. And again, and again, until only shreds of wood separated the holes.

"You know, that door will just go back to the way it was at midnight." Janus sat on the edge of Jaz's bed, hands folded on his knees.

Bracken started back, blinking. "I… don't care."

"I don't blame you for being angry. She should have told you."

Bracken scowled at him through the broken door. "You said you knew where she was. You let me think she was alive too."

"In a way, she is."

"Stop it."

Janus raised a hand. "Hear me out. As you've seen in Jaz's case, death is not always final."

Bracken couldn't help sneering at this. "If you're going to say something about an afterlife, don't." He turned away from the door, and found Janus standing behind him. He jumped back, bumping the demolished door. A glance into Jaz's room showed it was empty.

"You are not the only one who has lost someone dear to them. Jaz and I have been trapped here much longer than you have, and lost people much dearer." Janus gestured for him to follow, gliding away into the area where the brick hallway opened into a proper basement.

"I doubt that." Bracken followed him. The basement was lighted by overhead lamps that hung from long chains fixed to the ceiling. Two columns of metal shelves stood in the center of the room, making an aisle to the back wall. The ones nearest to him held coffee supplies. Bracken followed Janus down the aisle to the back of the basement.

The shelves there were even fuller than the front ones. They held all kinds of things, most of which had nothing to do with coffee: deck chairs, broken mirrors, coils of rope, boxy shapes he couldn't identify, piles of clothing, dishes, toys, books, appliances, containers — there was no end of junk. The last shelves were overflowing, the floor between them and the wall heaped with even more junk. It was all covered in thick dust.

"Welcome to the emotional distance corner."

Bracken shied away from Janus, who was suddenly standing beside him. "Stop doing that!"

Janus smiled depreciatingly. "Sorry. Again. It's kind of unavoidable."

Bracken scrutinized him. Janus didn't seem very sorry. If anything, he sounded amused. "Are you a ghost?"

"You could say that. When I was trapped here, I was separated from my physical body. I don't get around by walking, as you and Jaz do."

"Did Mr. White-Hair trap you too?"

"Mr. White-Hair?"

"Jaz said that's who trapped her here when her world was destroyed. A white-haired man."

"Ah. No, I was trapped in another way. There was a battle in my world. I lost and the… we'll call them magicians… of my world attempted to imprison my soul. They didn't quite succeed; as you can see, part of me ended up here. I can't leave until my body and the rest of my soul are freed."

"I heard that you're supposed to have two faces. That you're a powerful god, or something," Bracken tried to remember what Oz had called him. Luminary? Loamata?

Janus smiled. The warmth of it didn't enter his strange eyes, if such a thing were even possible. "That's an interesting take, certainly."

"So it's not true?"

"What do you think?"

"I think no one tells me enough."

"What do you wish to know?"

Bracken clenched his fists at his sides. "I want to know what happened to my aunt."

"The answer to that is not as simple as you might think. Come." Janus led Bracken away from the junk pile, between two shelves until they reached the wall on the left side of the basement. He didn't walk so much as slide, his feet not quite coming in contact with the floor. A light clicked on above them automatically, illuminating the area.

Bracken's eyes widened as he saw what covered the wall.

They were photographs. Thousands of them, separated by distinct color schemes into seven thick columns, from the ceiling nearly all the way to the floor.

Bracken walked slowly along the wall, looking at the faces, places, streets, fields, lakes, rivers, and forests that made up the whole; bits of life framed by countless viewfinders, passed to Jaz and added to these seven windows she'd made for herself; a view of all the things she couldn't touch; a map of everywhere she couldn't go.

"Look here." Janus touched a photo in the third column of an old man with spectacles. "This was taken in Grayson Gulch, world three." He moved down to another segment and touched a different photo of the same old man, without spectacles and wearing different clothes. "This one was taken in a city called Langston, in world five."

"Did he travel with Jaz too?"

"He did not." Janus's finger moved to a picture within the same column of a red-haired woman with freckled skin and a familiar smirk. "You should recognize her."

Bracken leaned close to it. "That's Aja."

"Correct." Janus moved back down the wall and pointed to another picture. "And this?"

"Aja again. But…"

"But in world six." Janus glided back the way they had come, stopping to tap another picture. "And now in world three. This is the version of Aja that you met."

"The version of…"

"Each of these seven worlds is a variation of the others. And variations of nearly each person in each world exist also."

"How does that even happen?" Bracken asked slowly, suddenly finding it hard to breathe.

"There are many theories. Some think each time a major point in history occurs, the turning point produces separate timelines following the possible outcomes. Others think that each world was created simultaneously and developed its own timeline independently of the others." Janus shrugged. "It doesn't matter how they exist, only that they do. This is good news for you though."

"Why?"

Janus slid away to the segment he called world six, and tapped another photo. Bracken went to look, and stopped breathing.

Sadie smiled out of the photo, her brown hair braided neatly back, her shoulders wrapped in a lacy shawl. "Your aunt exists in more than one world too. Even if one life is extinguished, others remain."

Bracken reached out and touched the photo, brushing her familiar face, and was able to breathe enough to whisper, "Which world is six?"

"Saturday. Two days from now." Janus was suddenly close beside Bracken. "I'll help you find her, if you'll help me get free."

23

Compartmentalizationism

Before Bracken could answer, Jaz's voice echoed through the basement. "Bracken? Hey, listen… you were right, okay? I should have told you…" Her voice, which was unusually gentle, trailed off into silence.

Bracken edged along the wall toward the front of the basement, past the shelves, until he could see Jaz. She was staring at her demolished door.

She turned when he cleared his throat. "There you are."

When Bracken stayed where he was, Jaz walked over to him. "Listen, I wanted to show you something. I should have shown it to you before, I just—" She stopped short when she reached Bracken, looking past him at Janus. Her voice instantly hardened. "Janus. What are you doing?"

Janus said calmly, "We were talking about Bracken's aunt. You remember the one…"

Jaz marched over to Bracken and grabbed his arm. "Don't talk to him, Bracken. I told you he's dangerous."

"He seems fine," Bracken observed.

"They always seem fine," she snapped, pulling him along the wall toward the stairs.

Janus stayed behind, watching bemusedly. "I was simply trying to help…"

"He showed me Sadie," Bracken said as he was towed along.

Jaz stopped, and he almost bumped into her as she spun to face him. "That isn't Sadie! Not the Sadie you knew."

Bracken glanced back, at Janus and the wall of pictures. "It's better than nothing, which is all you've given me."

Jaz's mouth formed a few words silently, her eyes large with anger. Finally she settled on, "Fine. You wanna see something, I'll show you something."

She pulled Bracken upstairs, stopping before the padlocked door between the basement and bathrooms. She undid the padlock with a key produced from her vest pocket and threw the door open.

The room was the size of a large closet. Light shone in from behind them, illuminating more metal shelves lined with thick binders, and a wood floor that stopped in the middle of the room before a deep shadow. Jaz stepped inside and reached above her head, pulling a thin chain. A light bulb clicked on, illuminating the rest of the room.

"This is where I keep the records of my time here. Mine, Sadie's, and other people's." Jaz pointed at metal shelves that covered three walls of the room, lined with binders, journals and notebooks. "I keep the most recent records in the daily binders. Everything else goes in here."

Bracken walked into the dark little room, stopped at the edge of a short drop-off and peered down. "Are those train tracks?"

"Yes." Jaz went to the shelves, searching for a certain binder.

Bracken hopped down, wincing as his bare feet crunched gravel, and stepped between the dark iron rails that ran from one wall to the other, parallel to the platform. "They don't go anywhere."

"Nope." Jaz pulled a binder from the shelf and flipped through it, coughing when dust rose up into her face.

"…why do you have a room with tracks that go nowhere?"

"Beats me. They were probably part of a service tunnel attached to the original building when The Defiant was taken out of my home world."

"Weird." Bracken stepped back onto the platform and inspected the binders on the shelves. He pulled one out and opened it. Photographs lined the pages in neat columns, captioned by different styles of handwriting. On some pages there was just a line or two beneath the photos; on others, words filled cross-sections of white space, curving up and down the margins.

Jaz looked over from the binder she held. She reached over to the one Bracken held and tapped a picture of a young man with a round, freckled face and dark wavy hair, wearing a jacket identical to Sadie's.

"Sadie helped me collect pictures too. We'd sit up at night sometimes and organize them. She did most of the albums on the bottom shelves."

Jaz's finger traveled down to the photo beneath, where the young man and Sadie sat together at one of the tables, heads bowed over something between them. "She made friends a lot easier than I did…"

"Who's with her in the picture?"

"Davin. He's a… he was a friend of hers. Of ours. You might meet him later." Jaz cleared her throat and took the binder from him, replacing it with the one she was holding. "Anyway, that's not important right now. Look at this."

Every picture in this album showed carnage: Cities on fire, streets broken by craters and smoking rubble, bodies in mass graves. Not all of the bodies were whole.

Bracken glanced away from the images. "What is this?"

"This is what Janus's kind did to the world before he became what he is now."

"He did all of that?"

"He had help. There was a huge battle between his kind, the Lumenatra, and the people who tried to seal away their powers, to keep them from destroying the world."

Bracken glanced backward through the open door. Across the café, the pristine street and buildings were visible through the windows. "When did all this happen?"

"A long time ago." Jaz was focused on a man in one of the photos, standing near a mass grave. His face, framed by straight black hair, was obscured by smoke or dust. A long dark coat was draped over his shoulders, sweeping back like long wings. It reminded Bracken of Tuoni the Raven from Sadie's stories — a winged being that guided the dead to the netherworld. A girl with a nice figure, wearing a skirt and striped stockings, stood beside the man. Her face too was out of focus.

Bracken studied the picture for a moment. "It seems pretty bad. But you can't blame Janus for fighting back, can you?"

Jaz shot him a hard look. "You're not actually defending him. I know you're not that ambivalent."

"Wouldn't you fight if someone was trying to capture you?"

"Bracken — they nearly destroyed an entire world." Jaz leaned toward him intently, almost dropping the binder she held. "And that's not the only thing he's—"

"Yeah, a long time ago. How do you even know that it happened the way you think it happened?"

"I was there!"

"You were here," Bracken corrected, pointing at the floor. "In The Defiant. A long time ago. And you don't have the best memory, let's face it."

Jaz slammed the binder shut. "Excuse me?"

Bracken felt her rage like physical heat, but he pushed on. He was angry too. "You don't. You don't even remember things you did yourself."

"Like what?" she asked, teeth clenched.

"Like photographing that stupid Sassacus book."

"You did that."

"Yeah, and *you* did. I'll show you." He closed the album he was holding, set it on the floor and left her standing in the room while he went downstairs.

In a moment, he returned with the aged packet of envelopes, which he shoved into her hand.

She shuffled through the photos. "Please. This is what you—" Her face suddenly fell blank as she stared at the photo of the tome's cover.

"It was in your office. Beneath the binders."

Jaz's mouth hung open, as if she were about to speak but forgot how. Her violet eyes stared down at the photo, widening to the point of making her look manic. She let the binder fall heavily to the floor by her feet, turned slowly and walked into the café, holding the envelope at her side. She sat down at the counter with her back to him, holding the pictures in her lap.

Bracken watched her, feeling only somewhat guilty. "You brought it on yourself," he muttered, returning to the binders on the shelves. If she hadn't been trying to forget Sadie, which she clearly had done by shoving all records of Sadie's time here into a locked storage room, things like that packet of photos probably wouldn't have also been forgotten.

Bracken searched the binders for world six, the world Janus said the other Sadie lived in. If Homburg was Monday, then Pucheon was Tuesday, Grayson's Gulch was Wednesday, and Houzai — today — was Thursday. The remaining three worlds were called Langston, Vasencea and Kysoto. Bracken couldn't remember which of these belonged to which day, so he started with a Langston binder. It contained many photos of bizarrely dressed people, and a fair amount of news clippings with headlines such as, 'Rebel Yeller Strikes again!' and 'Unmasking the Masked Devil.'

Kajaani would like these for her own newspaper, Bracken thought.

In the middle of the album were several loose photos of Jaz and a young man with blond hair and silver-blue eyes. He had a friendly grin. They sat close together at a table in The Defiant. Jaz looked exactly as she did now, except smiling. The young man's arm was around her shoulders in some of the pictures, and the way she leaned into him showed she was quite all right with that.

It was interesting, but not what Bracken was looking for. He flipped through to the end, saw no pictures of Sadie, returned the binder to the shelf and moved on to the Vasencea albums. The photographs in the first album he chose showed a large, ornate city with a lot of brickwork and towers, obscured by thick yellow fog. Bracken skimmed over the photos of architecture, focusing on the ones featuring people. Here was a picture of a serious-looking youth with dark brown hair and piercing eyes. He wore a familiar blue jacket with wide lapels, a patch depicting a brown bird in flight visible on one sleeve. Beneath this photo was a notation:

Davin, first day at Vasencea Academy.
Looks great in uniform!

So that was Davin, Sadie's old friend. Bracken turned the pages slowly. There were several pictures of Davin alone and also with other young men in similar blue jackets. Between two pages, Bracken found a loose piece of paper with neat writing in blue ink:

It never rains in Vasencea. Davin doesn't know
what it even looks like. He's never even seen
a rainbow! I showed him one out of a magazine
I brought with me but he thought it was fake. So
I took a picture from a rooftop across from The
Defiant next time I was in Homburg...

Bracken's breath caught as he realized whose words he was reading. He looked up from the paper that was suddenly trembling in his unsteady fingers and stared, wide-eyed, at the wall for a few moments, then returned to reading, much slower this time:

> *I showed him all my sketches for the book, and he said he could help me put them together. I told him it's a gift for my nephew. He doesn't know the truth about Jaz…*

Suddenly, he realized what book this referred to. He clutched the binder against his chest and raced downstairs into Sadie's room. There, on the desk, were the sketches he'd seen on his first day: birds and boxy shapes, and a figure wearing a crown. The sketches had seemed vaguely familiar then, but now Bracken remembered why.

They were part of a story that Sadie had told him, which evolved with each visit and each telling, one of her many fairy tales: The Brown Bird and the Trickster King. It was about a bird that wanted to travel over the mountains to a new home, but her wings couldn't get her there. She met a magician — who turned out to be the king of tricksters — who offered to give the bird new wings in exchange for performing a task for him. Bracken had loved the story, but had never learned how it ended.

Bracken looked at every piece of paper on the desk, studying every sketch and written line, though most of the writing was scratched out and rewritten many times, as if Sadie had been composing the story, trying out ideas but not liking most of them. If she had completed the story, it was somewhere else. Perhaps with this Davin fellow.

Bracken was electric with excitement. He forgot about Jaz brooding upstairs, about everything that had happened since that morning — which felt like weeks ago. There was only this new discovery.

For the next few hours, he searched every page in the Vasencea binder, determined to learn everything about the place, about Davin, about Sadie's activity — everything. He might have even succeeded, if he had not eventually fallen asleep.

He awoke sometime during the night to Jaz shouting outside his bedroom.

24

The Collector

There were certain things Jaz would never forget.

The day she met Athamas.

The day Sadie died.

The day a certain man, while bleeding out on her floor, made a deal with one of Janus' kind and was granted a new life in one of the other seven worlds.

And the day that Janus became trapped in The Defiant.

He'd looked different then. His hair was black. His square eyes were black tunnels in his head, instead of gray, with red sparks gleaming in their depths. His arms — all four of them — ended in six-clawed hands. Some of the claws were missing at that point, bloody tips remaining, and a few of the fingers had been sliced off. But it was him. The whole being of Janus, the godlike Lumenatra who had pulverized entire cities to dust. Cut armies to pieces. He'd even boiled a sea or two—

Or was that one of his own kind, one that he had betrayed?

Anyway, that was how the war on World Four — Thursday — had started. Janus and a few of his fellow Lumenatra had convinced the denizens of the world that they'd infiltrated (or did they invade? Or maybe they were exiled from their own dimension…?) that two of them were too dangerous, destructive, to be allowed to roam free in the world. Janus and his brethren — they called each other 'brother' and 'sister,' though they seemed to also be in paired relationships — showed the mortals how a Lumenatra could be caught and sealed away in a mortal vessel.

Naturally the mortals, realizing how very powerful the Lumenatra were, decided that all of these beings should be sealed for the safety of all. For a time, the entire world was at war, some fighting for the Lumenatra, whom they considered patron gods; most fighting for the world they wanted to protect from the same gods.

Eventually, and at the cost of countless lives, the mortals succeeded in this effort. And Janus was one of the last to be sealed. Jaz remembered that moment particularly well: it had happened inside The Defiant.

Perhaps 'well' was an overstatement. She remembered… that it had happened. The exact memory was muddled and nonsensical in parts, like a dream that lingered in wakefulness.

Windows turning to black portals. A monster with four arms and claws for hands exploding out of the espresso machine. A pool of blood on the floor, forming into a smaller version of a vampiric woman who stood and sipped from a tiny teacup she'd pulled from inside her tall hat. The monster's claws raking down Jaz's arm as he was pulled, stretched by an invisible force toward a humanoid figure, his prison and vessel, outside. Herself, screaming at him, begging to be released from The Defiant. The monster stretching, thinning, snapping away. A vague shadow outline lingering in his place, then sinking into the floor.

She discovered what became of that shadow several nights later, when she found it gliding back and forth in the basement, wringing its hands and moaning like a proper ghost. The monster — the Lumenatra, rather — had managed to peel a tiny bit of his being away as he was being captured, and stick it in The Defiant. That bit was Janus. And he was useless.

Oh, he had power. Incredible power, even though it was just a fraction of what his whole being could access. He just couldn't apply it to anything outside of The Defiant's walls. And he couldn't apply it to any sentient being without its permission.

He had no idea what had become of the rest of him, but he guessed that the human vessel where his essence had been stashed might resemble the human form he often took when interacting with mortals: a man with a young face and white hair.

That was the only detail he and Jaz had to go on. That, and that the locations and identities of the vessels were probably recorded somewhere, by Sassacus scribes whose life goals were to record everything of note that happened anywhere in their world. That faction in itself was a neat little setup by one of Janus' fellow Lumenatra before they too were sealed away. A few of the Lumenatra had little failsafes such as this in place. The Defiant had been Janus' failsafe, but he was unable to escape before he was sealed. Now he was just as trapped as Jaz was.

"The collector collected by his collection," Jaz muttered as she bent over an open photo album cradled in her lap. The words weren't hers, she was fairly certain. She couldn't remember where she'd heard them. Still, they were accurate.

Jaz pushed the album onto the floor and stood. She paced, stepping over the other binders and photo albums that she'd brought from the storage room into the basement, where there was enough floor space to spread them out.

The photos in the albums spanned a long, long history of years, but hours of staring at them had brought Jaz no closer to finding the point in time that she had taken the photographs Bracken had discovered.

"I did not take those pictures. I didn't… right?" She paused and looked around the basement. It was empty except for herself, the loaded shelves, and the large metal roaster that occupied its own corner to her right.

Janus, of course, was not to be seen, but that didn't mean he wasn't watching. Janus was an observer, and only showed himself when something was interesting enough to warrant the effort, or if there was something to be gained from it.

Jaz spoke as if he was somewhere nearby anyway. "Why didn't you say something about the pictures then? I'm sure you knew about them. We're not exactly in team mode right now, but come on! You want out as much as I do…"

Jaz continued to pace, staring down at the open binders and albums, dragging her fingers through her hair repeatedly. "They probably didn't have what you wanted. But why not? Or are they not complete? Did I start getting pictures and not finish? But when? When?! I didn't get this book before, right? Right?"

Her shout filled the basement, then flattened into silence. Jaz growled and kicked at one of the albums, flipping it over. "Janus! Janus, answer me, dammit!"

She kicked another album, and it skidded across the floor, bumping into one of the roaster's metal legs with a muted bang.

"Jaz?"

She stopped mid-kick and turned to see Bracken, standing in a disheveled state at the corner of his bedroom wall, blinking sleepily at her. She'd forgotten his room bordered the area by the roaster, and his bed was on the other side of the wall where she stood.

"Yeah, what?"

"Are you okay?"

"I'm great. Fantastic."

Bracken rubbed his eyes sleepily and looked at the binders arrayed across the floor. "What are you doing?"

"Spring cleaning. What's it look like?"

Bracken blinked at her, eyes wide and dark and so… sad. He'd covered his grief with anger and denial, but she was too familiar with grief to be misled by emotional masks. And she was too scared of how close she was to breaking down over Sadie's death also, even after — how many years? Five? And he'd only lost her a few months earlier, by his time. She'd wanted to protect him from having to live with that pain. Stupid. He would have found out eventually. She'd only made finding out worse.

Jaz realized she was staring at him while these thoughts ran through her head. She checked herself and shrugged, gesturing at the envelope of pictures lying atop one of the photo albums. "Sorry. I'm… trying to figure out when I took those pictures. Or if I had someone bring them here, or…" She rubbed her fingers through her hair again, though it was already standing out from her head like a close blue cloud.

Bracken sighed. Then he edged forward and crouched by the envelope. "Can I see?"

"Sure. Whatever." Jaz slid down the wall and pulled her knees against her chest.

Bracken picked up the envelope and shuffled through the photos. "There must be a reason you hung onto them for so long. I'm sure we'll figure it out."

We. How long had it been since she'd heard that, outside of the context of herself and Janus? Not since Sadie. The thought made her heart ache.

Of all the faces she was lucky enough to remember out of her long history, Sadie's was one that still touched a deep emotional chord in Jaz, a static point along a blurred timeline that no longer seemed attached to time, but to herself. A point she could never again see. A point that Bracken sometimes resembled, for all the chaos he caused since he'd arrived. Jaz watched his profile as he squinted at a photo. He was so willing to help. And so damn polite. She'd forgotten how politeness permeated his species. Politeness, loyalty, curiosity — all qualities she didn't possess in great quantity. That didn't seem to matter to him though. It certainly hadn't mattered to Sadie.

She realized she was staring again and dropped her forehead onto her knees. "There's probably nothing of use in those pictures. That's why I forgot about them. There's nothing there, and I'm never getting out. I am. Never. Getting out."

Bracken frowned at the picture in his hand. "Jaz…"

"It's just a game I play with myself, see. Just passing the time here. Endless time… endless… endless…"

"Jaz." Bracken scooted back until he sat beside her. "There are pictures of more than one book in here."

She raised her head and looked at the picture he held up. It showed the cover of a tome, but it was a different color than the one she'd borrowed, and the etchings across the cover were also different.

"I didn't take time to look through all of them before. I just saw the ones that matched the book I was photographing, and the cover…"

Jaz squinted at the picture in her hand, then took the envelope from Bracken and rifled through them. A few had been put in backwards. Jaz pulled out one of these and saw writing across the back. "Oh…"

Bracken straightened. "What?"

Jaz glanced at him. "I didn't take these. I think Sadie did." She showed him the back of the photograph. "That's her handwriting."

Bracken sat up straight, grinning. "She did? Wow… when? And why? Was she looking for Mr. White-Hair too?"

"Who? Oh… no." Jaz rested her head back against the wall and closed her eyes. "For a doorway generator."

"That thing Oz mentioned. I remember. So it…"

"Creates doorways, to wherever. She was hoping it would create one I could use, to get out of here."

"Okay… so, maybe this means she found it."

"She didn't."

"How do you know?"

"Because I'm still here."

Bracken lowered the pictures to his lap and stared down at them.

"I told her it was pointless. I told her so many times. But she was sure it was real. So sure. She searched for it right up to the day she died, and never—"Jaz's throat constricted, cutting off her next words. She stood, shoving a binder out of her way with her foot. "Forget about the pictures. They're pointless."

"Jaz—" Bracken glanced up at her.

Jaz shook her head, rubbing away tears that stung her eyes. "I'm going to bed."

"But there's more writing on the backs of these. Don't you want to at least—"

Jaz was already moving past him to her room. "Look through them if you want. Put the binders away when you're done."

25

Hello, Friday…

Bracken woke with a mild jolt to loud music thumping overhead. He blinked a few times at the ceiling. He vaguely remembered returning to his room when Jaz had gone to hers, and staring at the photos until he'd fallen asleep, sitting up on his bed. Bracken rubbed his face with both hands and stood. Then he yelped as the binder, which had been on his lap when he fell asleep, slid off and hit his foot. He picked it up and dropped it on the bed and then went upstairs into the café. Jaz was moving about the workspace with half-closed eyes, unloading white cappuccino cups from the dishwasher and stacking them on top of the espresso machine. Sarcastic rock resounded through the café, a male voice singing about dragons and beasts, drowning out Jaz's words when she spoke.

Bracken put a hand to his ear. "What?"

Jaz flicked a knob on the radio, and the music faded. "You didn't lock up," she repeated. When Bracken looked confused, she waved a hand toward the alcove where the door to the storage room stood open.

"I… forgot. The binders are still downstairs."

"Bring them up and put them in the storage room, will you? I'll get breakfast." Jaz felt in her vest pocket and came out with a key, which she dropped on the counter near him. "Use this to lock it up when you're done." She grabbed two silver pitchers from the dishwasher with one hand, fumbled and dropped them both. They bounced and rolled over the floor, clanging loudly. Jaz dismissed them with an impatient gesture and latched onto a kettle instead.

Bracken had a sinking premonition what breakfast would consist of. He went back downstairs, gathered up the photo albums Jaz had left on the floor, and deposited them in the storage room. His body felt heavy and sluggish, his legs not so much bending as wobbling as he moved. When he finished with the albums, he went into the workspace and stopped before the pastry case. He rested his forehead on the glass, looking at a pile of scones. "I haven't figured out anything from the pictures yet. I'll try again later. Most of the notes Sadie wrote don't make any sense."

Jaz didn't answer, but she didn't tell him to shut up either, so Bracken pushed on. "It would help if you could translate the, um, Sassacus text in the pictures. I bet Blaise's translator would work on them. He said it will translate anything."

"He meant anything in his world, not anything literally. Stop touching the pastry case. You're smudging the glass." Jaz smacked the faucet, shutting off the water, and dropped the kettle on a heating element.

Bracken lifted his head and rubbed at the glass with his fingers, which only made a bigger smudge. "Don't worry about it. If it doesn't work we'll figure something else out."

"I'm not worried," Jaz grunted, yanking Thursday's cash drawer out of the tray and replacing it with Friday's.

Bracken sighed and gave up. He looked to the windows. Dawn brightened the sky between skyscrapers that crowded out most of the blue, allowing only thin strips to show between them.

Jaz went into the kitchen and came out with a box of maple scones. Bracken took one with a small sigh. He missed having a normal breakfast, or at least meals that included vegetables. Jaz seemed to thrive on pastry and caffeine alone.

They ate the scones and sipped at some strong, nutty coffee that Jaz said was called Black Ivory, sitting side by side at the counter. Friday's binder lay open between them.

"These records are more like snippets," Bracken said, turning the pages. "Did you get bored and throw all the pages on the floor and then only put half of them back? Because that's what it reads like."

Jaz slouched over her plate, swirling the last of her coffee in the bottom of the mug. "Don't read them if you don't want to. Friday doesn't have much structure."

"I don't see how you can read them."

"I don't need to anymore. Occasionally I'll write a note if something important is happening." She glanced habitually at the window.

"This is almost gibberish. It may as well be in code."

Jaz popped the last corner of scone into her mouth and spoke around it. "Sorry my record keeping doesn't meet your high standards."

Bracken had finished his first scone and started on a second. It wasn't ideal food, but he was quite hungry. "It's for you as much as anyone. What if you forget who 'Rfeg' is? Or how many bottles of—" He squinted at the page "chocolate syrup go in Bingo Capkicker's monthly order? That's a fun name. I hope he comes in today."

Jaz grunted and refilled her mug.

"I want to see what someone who orders ten pounds of rock sugar and sixteen bottles of amaretto syrup looks like," Bracken persisted.

"An overstuffed chair wearing a waistcoat. He's not until next week." Jaz glanced again at the windows, watching someone pass by.

Bracken looked too, and almost choked.

He blinked twice, swallowed a mouthful of scone, and said, "That guy is dressed like a beetle."

"Yep."

"And what's she supposed to be?" Bracken pointed to a passing woman draped in sparkling robes and carrying a thick bronze staff. Multiple colored orbs were tucked into her tall hairdo, and a line of gold stars dangled from her earlobes.

"Small coffee with a 'dusting' of cream," Jaz said, connecting drink to name. "Starweaver."

Bracken scoffed. "Are you serious?"

"Yes." Jaz went to the row of siphons and prepared coffee in one.

People passed the windows intermittently, looking as people do when coming home after a grueling night shift, except these people wore costumes.

Eventually, one of them entered The Defiant. He wore a black turtleneck shirt, black slacks and a ski mask pulled over his face. Bracken glanced at him, then at Jaz, unsure if the masked man had come to buy coffee or empty the cash register. Jaz didn't flinch.

"Hi, Simon," she said, watching coffee drain from the top vessel into the bottom.

Bracken glanced down at the binder: 'Single-Siphon Simon' was marked down as 'Customer #1. 6:08/6:14 am'.

"Hey, Jaz. What's the coffee of the day?" Siphon Simon pulled off the cap, revealing curly blond hair.

"Black Ivory." Jaz caught Bracken's eye and nodded toward the storage room, which was still unlocked with the door wide open. Bracken closed the door, locked it and handed the key to Jaz, who took it with one hand while she poured Simon's coffee with the other.

As Simon walked out with his drink, the man dressed like a beetle who had passed by earlier walked in. His costume was made of a rubbery black material, with long tentacles waving atop an open-faced mask covering his head and neck. He wore thick rubber mittens, which were either suited to grasping electrical conduits or removing things from hot ovens. He was munching a hand pie that smelled of pepperoni and rubber, grease dripping from the wax wrapper onto the clean floor.

He stopped in front of the register. "What flavors do you have?"

Jaz recited in monotone. "Vanilla, caramel, chocolate."

He frowned and wiped grease from his mouth with the back of one mitten. Some stayed at the corners of his lips. "You don't have hazelnut?"

"Sorry."

"That's a pretty common flavor."

Jaz just looked at him.

"I don't know what I want then. What goes with vanilla?"

Jaz half closed her eyes, inhaling deeply. "Do you prefer hot or cold drinks?"

"Uh…" He squinted at the menu, rubber feelers jiggling over his forehead. "Surprise me."

She sighed through her nose and poured him a cup of black coffee.

He tasted it and asked if it could be sweeter. She added vanilla syrup.

He tasted it and asked if it could be colder. She added some ice.

He tasted it and said it was too cold, and asked if she could add hot milk.

Jaz stared at him for a long moment. Her left eye twitched. "No."

The man-beetle blinked. "You can't?"

"I won't."

"Can't you just—"

"Go away. You're done." Jaz went to stand behind the espresso machine, leaving him at the register.

He scowled and raised one of his mittens, opening and closing his fingers and thumb like pincers. "I am not alone. I have many friends. Many friends who will convince you to give me what I want."

Jaz folded both arms on top of the espresso machine, her expression tepid. "Do you now."

A scratching along the windows drew Bracken's attention.

He gasped and sidled up to Jaz, tugging the edge of her vest. "Jaz…" He pointed at the windows.

Beetles. Hundreds of beetles. They swarmed from seemingly nowhere, crawling up the panes in a near-solid mass of legs, bodies and antennae. In moments they were halfway up the windows. A mass of them were seeping in under the doors.

The man-beetle cackled, still wagging his mittens in the air. "You see! You can't stop the Beetler, coffee girl! They will do anything I tell them, anything at all! You are powerless! You—"

Jaz walked to the register. She pulled the shotgun from under the counter and leveled it at Beetler's face. "So if I shoot you, will they keep doing what you told them to do? Or will they go back to being just regular beetles?"

Beetler's eyes bulged. He lowered his hands slowly.

"That's what I thought."

Beetler glared. "This isn't over, cof—"

Jaz flicked the gun toward the ceiling and fired.

Beetler screamed. The beetles retreated en mass. They disappeared faster than they had appeared, in time with Beetler's dash out the doors.

Jaz replaced the shotgun, looking satisfied. "Frothing powered people…"

Bracken, who had hunkered behind the counter once the shotgun came into play, now straightened.

"Did he just call up a hoard of bugs?"

A new customer — this one on the stocky side with an unbuttoned flowered shirt, bell-bottom jeans and hair that flowed loose over his shoulders — entered the shop. He carried a wooden box about two feet tall. He sat down at a table near the doors and set the box on the table.

Jaz nodded, sparing a glance at the newcomer. "Some people here have abilities. Flying, calling up storms. Summoning bugs, apparently. It's really annoyi—"

A blast of bongos and rollicking organ music rocketed through the room. Bracken and Jaz turned — Bracken with a startled spin and Jaz with resignation — toward the music. It was coming from Flower Shirt's box. He rested his elbow and forearm across the top, grinning at the room.

Now in the doorway stood two very short people, each holding a door open with a gloved hand. Their heads barely reached the door handles. They wore identical black shirts and black knit hats. Each had a pair of black goggles, the woman wearing hers on her head and the man sporting his around his thick neck. Each held their door open with one hand and a bulging leather bag over one shoulder with the other.

Two more hands reached above their heads, pushing the doors open further. The hands belonged to a tall, athletic man dressed in fitted black clothing that contrasted with his pale hair and eyes.

The short pair swaggered toward the counter in time to the bongo fanfare and the man strode behind them, a king behind his tiny entourage.

Bracken stared at the show, his mouth slack, wishing he had his camera to hand. Jaz slouched back against the island, one foot against the door of the dishwasher, gently swirling the coffee in her cup. She scowled at the procession, violet eyes cut in half by her lowered brow, lifting the cup to her lips.

"Hello, Friday," she muttered over the rim.

26

A Company of Thieves

The man reached the counter and rested an elbow on it, leaning forward with a proud smile that Bracken thought was slightly familiar.

"Hi," he proclaimed over the music. "We just robbed a bank."

Jaz maintained her scowl. "Super."

"Yes we did," beamed the man, pointing at his comrades in turn. "Mose, Margo, the Jolly Pyro and yours truly."

Jaz's eyelids lowered in a very long blink. "Do we have to call you Yours Truly or is there an abbreviation?"

"The name is Sean, but you can call me whatever you like." Sean directed his smile at her.

Jaz raised an eyebrow, as if contemplating her options.

"Who is the Jolly Pyro?" Bracken asked.

Sean widened his grin and pointed back at Flowered Shirt who, still leaning on the hi-fi, lifted a bony hand in greeting.

"We call him J.P." Sean faced Jaz again, leaning both hands on the counter and swelling his chest. If he were a rooster he would have been crowing, not that anyone would have been able to hear it over the music. "We won't cause you any trouble, I promise. Just came to enjoy some good coffee."

"We're fresh out," said Jaz, contemplating the inside of her mug.

Bracken suddenly realized why Sean's smile was familiar. He was the one in the photos with his arm around Jaz. Bracken quickly glanced at Jaz, but she remained as stoic as she had been with the Beetler. She gave no indication of knowing Sean, much less being as close as they had seemed in the photos.

Sean continued to smile, settling onto a barstool. He raised a hand and gestured over his shoulder. J.P. turned down the volume to background level. "And we'll take four scones if you have them," Sean continued. "We're celebrating."

Jaz rolled her eyes and brewed coffee for five.

Bracken opened the pastry case and took out some blueberry scones. "Congratulations, I guess."

"Thanks. Couldn't have done it without my team." Sean helped Mose and Margo mount stools on either side of him. They watched Bracken with identical stares, like two guard dogs heeled beside their master. Bracken half expected Sean to scratch them behind the ears. J.P. came to the counter and sat beside Mose, setting the hi-fi on the counter top.

Sean produced several large bills from his pocket and slid them across the counter. "Thank you. We just need to lay low for a few hours until the hubbub dies down at the bank and then get out of town."

Bracken passed scones on plates to them. "You're not worried they'll come looking for you in here?"

Sean shook his head. "This isn't in the vicinity. They'll be checking hideouts of their enemies, none of whom live here. In about two hours someone else will stage a holdup and by tonight we'll be old news. This kind of stuff keeps bank owners in business. Insurance payouts pay the bills."

Jaz resumed leaning against the island while the coffee brewed, ignoring everyone. Bracken felt slightly sorry for Sean. Rudeness was part of Jaz's strange charm, but now it seemed she was just being mean for meanness' sake.

"I didn't know robbery was a career track," said Bracken.

"Live here a few weeks and you'll be doing it too, or something similar. Only jobs around here are crime or punishing it." Sean nodded to Jaz. "Or, making coffee, of course."

"What about anarchy?" Bracken asked, remembering Aton's bank demolitions and thinking he and Sean might have come to some mutually beneficial arrangement if they knew each other.

"This town thrives on corruption. Anarchy is probably not too far off, if certain kingpins go down," Sean said. "Personally, I like banks. They're a challenge, but predictable. I guess you could even say we work for them. They get back everything they lose and more from insurance."

"So you're entertained and paid, and the banks don't lose any money, so things don't get too sticky for anyone," said Bracken.

Jaz filled four mugs and passed them across in silence.

"It's a living." Sean gave the grin a rest, relaxing like a rooster settling own to enjoy his domain. "Personally, I don't need all the fanfare stuff, but since we don't wear costumes it's necessary. Nobody takes you serious in Langston if you don't stand out." He tasted the coffee. "Ah. That's the stuff."

"Glad you approve," Jaz said dryly, pouring the last of the coffee she'd made them into her own mug.

Sean jabbed a thumb over his shoulder. "We've been going to Scarro's, across the tracks. Their stuff tastes like wood."

"I only make coffee that I'd drink," Jaz said. "Wood is not my favorite flavor profile."

Sean nodded. "Who roasts it?"

"I do. I call it Black Ivory. Full city minus. I'm trying it out."

Bracken blinked. "Full city what?"

"It's a roasting term," Sean told him. He brought the cup beneath his nose and sniffed. "Nice nutty aroma." He took a sip, more deliberate than the first. "Mild acidity. Roasted hazelnut…" Sip. "Creamy body." Sip. Swallow. "Lingering spice in the finish. Love it."

Jaz blinked at first, surprised. Then as he continued his assessment, she brightened, almost smiling. "Thank you."

Now that she was acknowledging Sean as a sentient being, the atmosphere of the shop became considerably friendlier. Jaz mentioned something about her roast method, which Sean comprehended to her pleasant surprise. He praised the flavor profile, and Jaz actually smiled, brushing an escaped strand of hair behind her ear.

Bracken watched, fascinated and somewhat confused. Confused, because Sean was definitely the man in the photo, yet Jaz didn't appear to know him, and he seemed to be playing along. Fascinated, because this — coffee appreciation — was apparently be one of the few ways to win Jaz's approval. Bracken wondered if his aunt had hit it off with Jaz through photos, as he had, or through coffee. Sadie had never talked coffee like this on her visits to his family, but the nuances of coffee were not something one could slap on the unschooled mind with great results.

The coffee-centered courtship would have gone on, backed by quiet acoustic music straining through the hi-fi's speaker — a lighted window on the side read L'Appuntamento — but it was interrupted by Margo, who was watching the street. "We have incoming, boss."

Jaz smirked. "Boss, huh."

"Got an image to keep up." Sean twisted toward the windows. For the first time, his smile slipped.

A group of men in double-breasted suits were crossing the street, coming toward the shop. Several carried automatic weapons at their sides.

27

Eviction

Sean tensed, sitting straight on his stool. "Fatson."

"Crap." Jaz set down her mug.

Sean turned back to Jaz. "I'm sorry. We got away clean… I didn't know they'd send him…"

Jaz shook her head. "The bank didn't send him. He's a regular."

"Best get out of sight," said Mose, throwing back the last of his coffee and hopping down from his stool.

"Just to be safe," Margo agreed, setting down her empty cup.

Sean leaned toward Jaz. "I wouldn't normally ask this, but, you wouldn't have a storage room or something we could occupy for a couple of hours, by any chance? Just until the suits go away."

Jaz studied the approaching group with a growing frown. "Bracken, take them downstairs."

Bracken's mouth fell open. "Seriously? What about—"

"Put them in your room."

"My room? Are you kidding me?"

Sean blinked, turning to Bracken. "You live here?"

Jaz pulled Bracken aside before he could answer, lowering her voice. "Just keep them out of my office. There's nothing in your room they can't see."

"Or, we could make them leave." Bracken felt Sean watching them and lowered his voice further.

Jaz clenched her teeth, hissing through them. "Fatson is bad news, kid. Bad news. If you get these nice bank robbers killed, I'll kill you."

"That's a weird thing to say, after the way you've been acting," he returned, speaking softly.

"What way have I been acting?"

"You know…" Bracken tipped his head slightly back, indicating Sean.

"What, because someone finally comes here who knows something about coffee? Fates. Just take them downstairs, all right?"

"That wasn't what I— Fine. But if they find out all your secrets and this blows up on you, don't blame me."

"Don't let them find out and we'll be fine." Jaz glanced at the windows again and pushed him out of the workspace. "Hurry up!"

"Okay, okay." Bracken threw open the basement door and led the way downstairs. Sean came after him, the twins heeling on either side. J.P. came behind them carrying the hi-fi, which now changed its tune from romantic guitar to a spy theme.

"What did you do before you had the theme-music box?" Bracken asked, coming to the bottom of the stairs.

"J.P. mostly hummed." Sean looked at the nearest shelves, and then at the bulky roaster hunkered in quiet repose beyond the nearest lights to his right. "Look at that..." He took a step toward it but Bracken checked him with a hand on his arm.

"This way."

"Right. J.P., come back," Sean called.

J.P. had already approached a nearby shelf, which was full of vinyl records. He came back to them, thumbing over his shoulder at the records. "Nice collection."

"Don't touch anything," said Bracken, hoping J.P. hadn't noticed most of the titles were in languages not found in his world. "Jaz is obsessive with her organizational system."

He began to open his door, and saw the Vasencea binder on his bed, and photos spread across the blanket. He quickly closed the door. "Hang on. I have to... just a second."

He slipped inside and quickly shoved the binder into his backpack. He gathered up the photos into a loose pile and dropped them in the top desk drawer. Then, shoving the backpack far under the bed, he called, "Okay!"

Sean looked at him amusedly as he opened the door again, this time stepping back so they could enter. "Hey, if you need a minute to clean—"

A crash of furniture overhead and sudden yelling made them all jump. Images of tigers and blood splatter on cabinets shot through Bracken's mind.

Sean spun and would have started back upstairs, but Mose and Margo caught his arm, speaking at the same time.

"You can't."

"Fatson, remember?"

Sean's face was pale in the faint light filtering down on them, his arm stiffening as if to pull away.

"I'll go see what's up," Bracken offered quickly. "If she's in real danger I'll yell."

Bracken didn't trust them alone in the basement, but the crashing continued along with the sound of stomping feet. If Jaz died again he would be alone for the rest of the day, which didn't appeal to him. And even though it wasn't permanent, dying probably wasn't much fun for her either. He opened the door to his room and shooed them inside. "Don't steal anything. It's… got sentimental value."

Sean faced him from the middle of the room and spread his hands. "We won't take anything," he promised. "Go help her."

Bracken didn't believe they would stay there, but helping Jaz against the unknown assailants was more important than guarding bank robbers hunkered in his room. At least they weren't performing any demolitions. Bracken sprinted upstairs, expecting to see holes ripped in the floor and rubble strewn about.

There were no holes, no rubble. Just four men in black suits, tossing chairs and shoving tables out the open double doors onto the sidewalk. Jaz sat on the counter with her feet on two stools, sipping from her cracked coffee mug.

A fifth, stocky man in a light gray suit stood facing her, lighting a fat black cigar. He wore no hat. His reddish hair was cropped in a flat plane across the top of his head like a miniature, well-trimmed bush.

"What's going on?" Bracken came around the counters to stand beside Jaz.

"We're being evicted." She gave him a dry look.

Bracken leaned closer. "Is that even possible?"

"You bet it is," the shrub-haired man answered, gesturing with the lighted cigar as smoke floated in clouds around his head and shoulders. "And this time I'm making sure it happens."

"Sure, Fatson, sure." Jaz mimicked his gesture with her mug. "I'm more than happy to vacate."

Bracken barely caught the laugh that came over him at this, stifling it into a smirk instead.

Fatson's red skin reddened further. "You said that before. This time, you better scram if you don't want to eat bullets."

"You'd shoot a woman?" Jaz tsked and brought her mug to her lips. "Classy."

Fatson grabbed the mug and threw it across the room. It bashed into a wall and crashed on the floor in pieces.

Jaz clenched her jaw, her chest rising with a deep, slow breath. "That was my favorite mug."

Fatson stabbed a stout finger at her face. "I'll be back in the morning. If you're still here I'll decorate the walls with your brains."

He left his henchmen to see that the moving out proceeded as planned. Jaz ignored them and searched the floor for shards of her mug, collecting them in her apron pocket.

Bracken edged close to her and held out part of the curved handle. "We can't leave."

"Nope. But they don't know that." Jaz took the piece. "Thanks."

"The furniture they're throwing out the doors, can we get it back?"

"Nope." Jaz looked toward the windows. Chairs and tables made large piles on the sidewalk. Her eye twitched briefly. "I have a few tables downstairs that I've been hanging onto. Fatson has been coming by every couple of days, by his time, and he's getting frustrated that I'm not complying with his edicts."

"He keeps trying to throw you out and failing."

"Yeah. I was giving him Joli's anti-memory tea for a while, which was pretty nice. Don't have it today though." Jaz shot a pointed glance at Bracken.

"I said I was sorry, geez…"

Two henchmen approached, carrying semi-automatic rifles low at the hip, like they meant business but didn't want to try too hard at it. Bracken felt hopeful, but a look at their faces suggested their only thought in life was to carry out their leader's orders, over Bracken and Jaz's corpses if necessary. Jaz of course had nothing to worry about, but Bracken was still mortal.

"Boss wants everything gone," said Henchman One.

"Everything," confirmed Henchman Two.

"You mean the stuff downstairs. Sure." Jaz might have been taking their coffee order. "I'll have Bracken get started on it."

"We'll go with," said Two.

"He doesn't need help. I have four more employees downstairs. Bracken, tell them to help carry stuff out."

Bracken hesitated. "Are you sure that's—"

"Start with the junk in the back corner. Go on," she commanded when Bracken continued to hesitate. "It's time they earned their keep." She retrieved another shard of her cup from under an overturned chair.

"What are you going to do?" Bracken asked.

"I'll take care of things up here." She looked at Bracken hard and nodded.

"All right. You're the boss." He shrugged and went back downstairs.

Sean waited at the bottom, leaning against the wall. He straightened when he saw Bracken. "So?"

"That guy Fatson is evicting us. His guys are throwing the tables and chairs outside. Jaz is going along with it so no one gets hurt."

This didn't please Sean either. "Fatson is an insurance salesman, not a landlord."

"I get the feeling he doesn't care about details like that."

"Yeah," Sean mused. "Banks and museums under his watch are too dangerous for the average thief to hit. He likes to mess people up who try to steal from him."

"Did you steal from one of his banks?"

"No, I like keeping my life." Sean glanced up the stairs. "I don't like that he's here though. He doesn't care if he kills a man, woman or stray kitten that rubs him the wrong way."

"He just left," Bracken was happy to announce. "Just his guys are here right now."

"How many?"

"Four."

"All with guns?"

Bracken nodded. "Jaz said you should help carry some stuff out. There's a junk pile down here we can use. You can sneak off when you get outside. She told them you're her employees. They shouldn't bother you if you hurry."

"What about Jaz?"

"I'll watch out for her. Besides, you have loot to worry about."

Sean hesitated, as if torn between his career and an underlying streak of honor, then pushed off the wall and went to Bracken's room where his crew waited. Mose and Margo sat on the bed, legs dangling. J.P. was cross-legged on the floor beside the hi-fi.

"We have a slight change in plans," Sean said. "J.P., come with me and Bracken. Mose and Margo, you watch the loot. Bracken," he turned to Bracken, regaining his former commanding confidence, "Take us to the junk pile."

28

A Minor Infestation
of Henchmen

They went to the southeast corner of the basement where the junk rose like a mountain into the deeper shadow of the corner. Some of it was covered by a gray, dusty tarp with holes worn through here and there as if the tarp had been used for many things over many decades.

"Just grab whatever and carry it up." Bracken told them. He lifted a corner of the tarp and paused to cough in the ensuing dust storm before continuing. "Kill time until evening. Fatson's guys have to clock out sometime."

*

Bracken, Sean and J.P. walked, shuffled and moseyed up and down the stairs, leisurely carrying all kinds of items to the door and tossing them into the street.

Cars and pedestrians had trouble navigating the debris choking the streets and sidewalk, and every so often the flow of foot and motor traffic backed up, swirling around the piles until they found their way through and flowed onward and away.

"So, you and Jaz live here?" Sean asked as he and Bracken came downstairs together for another load.

"Yeah."

"Together?"

"Yeah."

"Oh."

Bracken glanced at Sean, and as realization came over him he said quickly, "Not together. Not like that. No. Just… roommates."

"Just roommates. That's nice."

"Yeah. Sometimes." Bracken wasn't about to bring up her insane mood swings, or her insanity in general. When Jaz was doing well, she was fine. Fun, even. She was kind, sometimes, in her own way. Like when she'd ordered in dinner for him in Pucheon, and made him tea the first night, and hot chocolate the second — both spontaneous acts, yet just what he'd needed at the time. And she did apologize for her tantrums and outbursts, eventually. Under normal circumstances he might have even enjoyed working for her.

And now that he thought about it, her insanity and mood swings didn't bother Bracken much. The insanity was kind of interesting and he could tolerate her temper. If she hadn't lied about Sadie...

"So... you just work for her?"

Bracken blinked. They had crossed the basement while he was thinking and now stood in front of the junk pile, which was by no means diminished.

"Yeah."

After a weighted pause, Bracken had another realization. "Yeah, just coworkers. Nothing more. I'm not into huma... I mean... we're related."

Sean's smile was faintly relieved. "She your aunt or something?"

"Yeah... great aunt."

"That's nice." Sean picked up an old suitcase with a broken handle. "It's good to work for family. I worked with my dad for a while before he passed on. They were good times."

Bracken picked up a heavy metal box with a window on one side, the glass obscured with brown splotches, and followed Sean through the basement, back upstairs.

It didn't surprise him that Sean seemed to fear he and Jaz were an item. Especially considering Jaz's behavior toward Sean when he first came in, pretending not to know him, and her dramatic shift in attitude toward him after they began talking. The girl was just plain confusing, that was what.

While her 'employees' emptied the basement, Jaz had stayed in the workspace, pulling things off shelves, wiping them with rags, then wiping the shelves, then replacing all the items and starting on another shelf. No doubt it was the deepest cleaning those shelves had had in some time. Fatson's henchmen were occupied watching Bracken and company come and go, and generally left her alone.

After tossing the box outside and watching it land with a tumbling crash, Bracken stole behind the counter to confer with Jaz.

She had left off the deep clean for a bit and was sitting on the counter by the espresso machine, gluing her mug back together. "How's the junk supply holding up?"

"There's still half a mountain down there. We could throw stuff out for a week before we get to the bottom of it." Bracken nodded toward the henchmen standing guard near the doors. "It's enough to outlast them, unless Fatson intends for them to become permanent residents."

Jaz squinted at her mug, pressing another fragment into place. "If they stay past midnight, they'll be permanent all right. Just not in any way that they define the term. Pretend to keep working so they don't come over here."

Bracken pulled several bottles of syrup from a bottom shelf and lined them up on the counter beside the register.

"Why not remove Fatson from his native territory and deposit him in tiger world as a gift to the bloodthirsty? Or better yet, use him as a shield."

Jaz shook her head. "That world is unstable enough without throwing a gangster insurance agent into the mix…"

Her words died away as she looked past Bracken.

Sean had just come up again from the basement. He strode over to join them, folding his forearms on the counter as he leaned toward Jaz. "We need a strategy. This isn't going to work forever."

"It will until tonight, which is all I need," Jaz said, holding up the mug to inspect her repair.

"When Fatson comes to drag you out? That's not a great plan," Sean said. He glanced at the henchmen and shuffled some stacks of napkins from one spot to another in a pretense of productivity.

"He can't drag me out," Jaz began, then stopped and glanced at Bracken. They both considered the consequences of Fatson being unable to drag her out the front doors, and then finding out why.

"You're just stalling for time," Sean said, coming behind the counter to stand beside Jaz. He pulled a stack of demitasse cups toward him, pretending to count them. "It won't get these guys out of here, or Fatson off your back."

Jaz picked up a shard of her mug and examined the edge.

"What do you suggest, I hit them over the head and hold them for ransom?"

"That's an idea, but what I'm thinking is we should find something Fatson wants more than this café that you could use as a bargaining tool. Something expensive and useful, like Vorpol armor."

Jaz scoffed. "I don't have Vorpol armor."

Sean faced her with a sly grin, leaning an elbow on the counter. "Are you sure about that?"

Jaz was not sure.

"So it's possible." Sean nodded vaguely toward the henchmen, who were splitting their attention between Jaz and Sean, and the heap of junk now blocking the sidewalk. "Anyway, we just need to get them interested enough that they let their guard down. Then we use this."

He took something out of his pocket and showed it to them behind the counter. It was a small, translucent black cube with a cloudy white sphere in the center.

"What am I looking at?" Jaz asked, after a glance.

"A minion maker." Sean said, with obvious pride.

Bracken looked to Jaz for an explanation but her face was blank.

Sean seemed disappointed. "You've never heard of the minion maker? Legendary weapon of the Death Lord? He amassed quite a few armies with it. Or, one like it. Mose made this one."

Jaz snorted. "The real lord of death doesn't make armies. He cleans up the aftermath."

Sean shrugged and returned the cube to his pocket. "Anyway. It's push-button hypnosis. Just flash this in their eyes, and you're their new boss. Or whoever they see first after their vision comes back."

Bracken whistled. "That's pretty cool."

"We use it on heists sometimes, when security is heavy. Just point and shoot. No chases, no fights, no fuss. Wears off in a few hours, which is more than enough time to send them to the nearest police station and turn themselves in. We do the same to Fatson when he comes back, and problem solved."

"I see," Jaz said flatly, rubbing at a smudge on the espresso machine's side. "So then I gather you want me to pay you to take care of my Fatson problem."

Sean looked wounded. "Of course not. I have plenty of money. What I need is somewhere to stash it after jobs. This place is ideal, or it will be once Fatson takes his eyes off it."

"I wouldn't trust a bunch of thieves in my basement, long-term," Jaz said, bunching her shoulders stubbornly. "I keep a lot of valuable equipment down there. The roaster, for instance."

Bracken nodded, backing up what he thought was a sound decision. The worst thing that could happen to the last of Sadie's things was being stolen and redistributed to the undeserving denizens of Friday's world. Or any world, for that matter.

"We don't want your equipment," Sean said. He picked up a demitasse cup, inspecting it for cracks. "We're bank robbers. We like to get our money direct from the source. And if we stow our loot here, it's in our best interest to keep you happy so that our hiding place stays a secret." He lowered the cup and met her eyes. "You have my word we won't steal from you."

A long look passed between them, Jaz's scrutinizing squint against Sean's reassuring smile. She shook her head, looking away, the match ending in Sean's favor.

"Fine," she said, "But I know people. If you steal from me, I'll take it out of your soul."

"Done." Sean nodded. He beckoned Jaz and Bracken closer. "Things are set downstairs. Just follow my lead." Sean straightened abruptly, pushing away from the counter and raising his voice. "I didn't sign up to move all that contraband for you. If you're not going to pay me what I'm worth, maybe these guys will."

The henchmen turned their attention — and their guns — toward Sean.

Jaz gave Sean a warning look, the universal silent command to *zip it*.

Sean continued, unzipped. "What? There's no point in hiding it anymore, Jaz. They're gonna find it anyway."

"Find what?" One of the henchmen came closer. He had tiny black eyes and a square mustache directly under his wide nose. Aside from the mustachio, his face and brushy haircut resembled Fatson's, so much so that they could have been brothers.

Sean turned to him, setting the demitasse down on the last free bit of counter space. "Vorpol armor, a whole set. Pants, jacket, helmet. Vintage stuff."

Two more henchmen came closer, eager for details. They all had similar features, though their hair was different cuts, and two of them had facial hair.

One of them wiggled his mustachio and gestured at Jaz. "That true?"

Jaz shrugged weakly and scowled at Sean.

"You guys don't know the gold mine you're onto here," Sean said. "Jaz is a master in black market trade. She's been fencing stuff for years. The coffee shop is just a front."

The men eyed Jaz with new suspicion.

Bracken stared at Sean, wondering how the man would react if he knew how close to the truth that claim was.

Jaz traded her scowl for a skeptical, bored expression. "If I had Vorpol armor, I'd be wearing it."

"Don't lie. I saw it in that pile of stuff you're keeping for next week's auction," Sean said. He motioned to the henchmen. "I'll show you."

The henchmen shuffled their feet, considering Sean and Jaz. Finally, Mustachio nodded and gestured with the barrel of his gun toward the basement door. Sean led the way downstairs, with Fatson's men close at his heels. Bracken and Jaz trailed after them.

29

Polymorphic Spree

Jaz clenched Bracken's arm. "If this doesn't work, if they get into my office, kill them," she said out the side of her mouth.

"With what?" Bracken asked, keeping his voice low and his head close to hers.

"I don't care. Turn your arm into a knife."

He grimaced. "I'm not gonna stick my arm through some guy's body. Yuck."

She tightened her grip. "If they get in there and take my stuff, I'll never forgive you."

They followed Sean and the henchmen across the basement toward the junk pile, like two gazelles following a pride of lions to the community watering hole.

"Do you really have Vorpol armor down here?" Bracken asked in a near whisper.

"No," whispered Jaz, then after a moment added, "Probably not."

"Probably?"

"People leave junk here and I throw it in the pile. I don't keep an inventory. But if someone left something as valuable as Vorpol armor I'd—"

"Sell it?" Bracken prompted.

"No, stupid. I'd wear it on tiger day."

"I bet Blaise would pay a lot for it."

"If I had it I'd keep it," Jaz told him.

"But you can't d—" The word 'die' stuck in Bracken's throat like piece of stale scone. He looked ahead and caught Sean's backward glance: the man could hear them.

Sean stopped at the base of the junk pile and eyed Bracken and Jaz through the pack of suits between them. Bracken coughed softly and tried to look vague. Jaz folded her arms, radiating irritation.

"It's in here, somewhere," Sean said, rummaging under said tarp. "Here!" He produced a thick yellow vest with rows of buckles across the front. "The rest of it is here too. Pants, helmet…"

All four of the henchmen stepped forward and peered at the jacket. Then four pairs of dark, mean eyes squinted at Sean.

"That's not Vorpol armor," Mustachio growled.

"It's not?" Sean turned it and inspected the swinging buckles on the front.

"Vorpol armor—" the henchmen lifted their guns to waist level "—is green."

"Ah. My mistake." Sean tossed the vest aside and stepped back, raising his hands. "Looks like things are about to get hairy."

All four men pivoted toward Jaz, Moustachio in the lead. "I knew you'd try something."

Jaz pulled Bracken behind her.

Sean ahemed and raised his voice. "I said things are getting hairy!"

A crowd of bright, popping flashes erupted between two shelves on their right. A blast of good-time funk, produced by J.P.'s hi-fi, resonated through the room.

Bracken hit the floor, pushed down by Jaz. The men turned toward the lights and opened fire. The shooting lasted about five seconds, then stopped abruptly as Mose and Margo descended from overhead, each holding a corner of the tarp like a floppy parachute. They came down over the men's heads, landing heavily. They knelt on the edges of the tarp as the men struggled, their heads misshapen lumps bobbing beneath the tarp. Sean whipped out a black ropelike object and whacked at the lumps through the tarp. J.P. emerged from the shadows between some shelves and waded in with his own black rope, thwacking and smacking.

The lumps dodged and bellowed at first, then clumped together. Four lumps became two. Then the two pushed together and became one very large lump. It rose higher, then a fist punched straight up, tearing through the tarp.

"Fates," Jaz groaned. "He's a polymorph!"

Fatson rose, huge and hulking, hands grasping the edges of the tear and ripping the tarp nearly in half. He caught Mose, then Margo as they attempted a flank attack and flung them in opposite directions. Mose disappeared between two shelves, tumbling into shadow. Margo flipped over in the air and landed on Jaz, just as Jaz found her feet.

The music stopped abruptly, the sound of Jaz's head smacking concrete like a final cymbal crash.

Bracken scrambled toward her, but was knocked away by Fatson's foot as the now-giant man advanced toward Jaz. Margo rushed at him, diving for his legs to trip him up. He wrapped one massive hand around her neck and pulled her off, holding her up like a kitten.

J.P. rushed in just in time to catch Margo as Fatson tossed her aside a second time. They fell against a shelf, knocking off bottles of syrup which crashed and splashed around them.

Fatson leaned down and grabbed Jaz by her hair. "I knew you'd try something. You always do something tricky to delay moving out. But not this time. I told you, this time you're leaving. Dead or alive."

Jaz clutched at his fingers, shrieking as he lifted her up. Her boots swung and kicked several inches above the floor. Sean rushed up with a long pipe, which he threw at Fatson's head as he brought the black cube up in his other hand.

The pipe glanced off Fatson's forehead. Fatson flinched. His skin rippled slightly, as if made of thick rubber. Still holding Jaz aloft, he side-punched Sean, who flew back and skidded across the floor, then lay still. The minion maker fell from his limp fingers and was crushed under Fatson's foot as the man walked forward, holding Jaz.

He clamped thick fingers around Jaz's neck and squeezed, letting go of Jaz's hair to punch at Bracken, who had launched up at him from the other side. Bracken bent snakelike around the thick forearm, up to Fatson's shoulder. Fatson shook his arm. Bracken latched on, growing needle-like spikes to dig in. He wasn't very good at this level of shapechanging, and Fatson's skin was impenetrable, but Bracken didn't know what else to do. Jaz was kicking her feet and twitching in Fatson's grip, her face a deep purple.

"I'm done playing games, girl," Fatson rumbled, pulling her contorted face close to his. "You're finished."

A shadow stirred at the far end of the room, near the stairs. It caught Bracken's eye over Fatson's shoulder as he bit down on the man's deltoid as hard as he could. At first Bracken thought it was Janus, finally stepping in to help, but the shadow formed into two wings stretching toward them, sliding along the edges of the shelves. A massive raven's head appeared between them. The silver curve of a scythe-like beak gleamed beneath the head, easily half the height of the room. This wasn't Janus. This was—

"Hel!" Fatson took a step back.

"Tuoni…" Bracken breathed. He looked just like Bracken had imagined he would, except…

A man emerged from within the shadow, walking silently beneath the massive beak. The edges of his long coat flared as he walked: first thick fabric, then the rough edges of flight feathers. His shoes were black, his pants deep maroon, his shirt white. His face was pale and narrow, coldly composed.

"What brings you here, Hel? Did you come for her soul?" Fatson shook Jaz; she gurgled faintly.

The man continued toward them. The shadow extended over and past him, pushing ahead eagerly. The scythe-shaped beak opened, separating into two curved blades. Bracken unwound himself from Fatson's arm and shrank away from the shadow, from the desire to feed radiating from the blades.

Fatson felt it too. "Here, take her! She's almost dead already." He threw Jaz toward the shadow.

The man flashed forward and caught her. Jaz slumped against him, heaving for air like a swimmer breaking out of deep water. The man held her in one arm, tipping his face down to look at her. "Are you all right?"

Jaz could only cough violently.

The man's eyes snapped up, locking with Fatson's. A red gleam shone in them, sparks ignited in darkness. "How dare you touch what is mine."

"I… I'm sorry! I didn't know you had—"

"I alone have claim to her soul. As I have to all." The man's voice was heavy, resonant, like a resined bow drawn across a base string.

Fatson backed away, holding his hands before him, staring at the points of the blades hovering above his head. He didn't seem to notice the man within the shadow. "Please, go ahead and take her. I don't mean to get in the way of your claim—"

The man's resonant voice sharpened in disgust. "I don't require your permission to take what is rightfully mine. Nor do I need it to claim you."

Fatson's back hit the wall behind him. Everyone else in the room who was still conscious shrank away as the man-and-shadow advanced, closing in on Fatson, who ducked his head, muttering about Hel's scythes and hooded eyes. It sounded almost like a prayer.

Bracken crouched on the floor, but he couldn't stop watching the man. Jaz remained leaning against him, clinging to his coat, held upright by his arm around her shoulders. His pale hand supported her head, fingers tunneled in her blue hair.

Fatson turned and pounded both fists against the wall. The bricks cracked, mortar crumbling, rolling down.

"Unfortunately," said the man, still advancing, "it is not your time yet. But I know where to put you until then."

Fatson screamed, a gross, guttural noise, clawing at the wall. The beak snapped down at him — *shhick*. Fatson's scream cut short as he and the bird-shadow disappeared. Only the man remained, staring hungrily at the place where Fatson had been. The man looked down at Jaz, who was looking up at him. The hunger intensified as he studied her face.

Finally he said, "Really, Jaz. Twice in one week? It's a bit much."

"It wasn't planned," Jaz croaked.

"He's just worried you'll try to get thrown into limbo, like you did that one time," said a female voice near the stairs. "Your un-deaths don't go unnoticed, you realize."

Bracken rose to his knees and peered toward the stairs. A pretty young female was sitting on the bottom step, one knee casually crossed over the other. She seemed to be a Morpha: she was texturizing a skirt and blouse, and the stripes on her legs which resembled stockings were clearly her own skin. Yet Bracken knew, somehow, she wasn't one of his species.

"I'm not…I promised…wouldn't…"Jaz said, still breathless.

"I'm just saying," replied the girl. "This place might suck but it's better than floating in limbo for eternity."

"Just, try to be more careful," the man cut in with a sigh. "There's a world war on Vitrol-5 I'm supposed to be handling at the moment."

Jaz nodded.

"And don't allow these people to cause any more trouble."

Jaz shook her head.

"I can make things quite terrible for them." The man hadn't acknowledged anyone else in the room, but this was clearly a warning.

"They're not causing trouble," Jaz said quickly. "Fatson was the only one causing trouble. We didn't know he was a polymorph. Anyway, he's gone now."

"If you're sure…" He seemed disappointed.

"Let's go, Athamas. That war won't clean up after itself." The girl stood and stretched, showing off a perfect figure.

Bracken tried not to stare.

"Yes, yes…" Athamas released Jaz, who stood wavering somewhat on unsteady feet. He appeared normal without the looming shadow, but the weight of it was still present.

Jaz looked up at him, unconsciously touching her swollen throat. "Come back when you're finished. There's cobbler…"

"I will." Athamas nodded to her and walked back the way he had come. His companion joined him as he reached her, and they went out, passing through the wall.

Jaz watched him go, then turned quickly, searching the room until she saw Sean, still lying on the floor. An expression of near panic flashed across her face as she hurried over and knelt beside him.

Her hands pressed to his neck, searching for a pulse. "Don't be dead… please don't be…"

Sean stirred, raising his head. "Not… not dead. You?"

Jaz sighed in relief, slumping to sit beside him. "Still alive."

Sean rolled onto his back, grimacing as he touched a swelling bruise above his ear. "Though I might wish for it come morning…"

"Don't say that." She looked down at him.

He smiled up at her, his grin crooked and painful.

Bracken slid down against a shelf to sit, rubbing his own bruises and staring at Jaz. She was giving Sean a look that, while it wasn't exactly same one she had given Athamas, it was definitely in the same category.

30

Dating for Immortals

Jaz sat on the counter, watching Sean and his gang carry tables inside, while supervising Bracken. "No, the tea goes on the left-side counter, third shelf down. Teapots on the shelf above. Careful! They won't respawn if you break them."

Bracken steadied the armload of teapots and placed them, more or less carefully, on the proper shelf. "Why not?"

"They're not original. Any object brought in from outside the shop won't reset like the original items. I got the teapots because the elves were complaining. They drink it by the pot, or not at all. Start on the mugs next."

Bracken sighed deeply, rubbing at an ache in his neck that had sprung up in the last hour, beneath the abrasions from being tossed around the basement by Fatson. He wasn't enthusiastic over his role in the cleanup efforts, but since he couldn't help Sean and company bring in chairs and tables from outside, he was relegated to indoor organizing, with Jaz supervising. Sean had insisted she rest after being nearly strangled to death. Bracken knew this was fair, but all this work was so exhausting.

"First we carry everything out, now we have to put it all back." Bracken collected mugs arrayed on the countertop. "I've basically spent an entire day carrying stuff."

"Welcome to Friday." Jaz stretched her legs out on the counter, crossing her ankles. Beside her, J.P.'s hi-fi was playing sultry piano jazz. The small window on the side read Easy Does It.

She rested her head back on the wall, watching Sean drag a chair from under a pile of colorful sweaters out on the sidewalk.

"By the way, why did you pretend not to know him?" Bracken asked.

"Sean? I don't know him."

"Yeah, you do. There are pictures of you two in one of the old binders."

Jaz sat up, looking shocked. "What?"

Bracken shrugged awkwardly, clutching a cluster of mugs in each hand. "You looked like you were pretty close in them, so I figured…"

Jaz hopped off the counter and went to the storage room. Bracken put the mugs away and moved on to stacks of napkins. He couldn't remember where they were usually kept, and there was no room on the shelves under the counters, so he hunted along the cupboards beneath the back counter along the wall. He opened one of these cupboards and a landslide of paper cups in long plastic sleeves spilled out onto the floor. He was busily trying to nudge and kick them back into place with his foot while cradling the napkins when Jaz returned, holding the photographs. She looked relieved. "That wasn't Sean. It was someone else. His father, I think."

Bracken ceased kicking at the cups. They slithered out again. "His father?"

"Yeah," Jaz scrutinized the top photo. "I'd have to check the records, but I wrote his name down on the back of the picture. Finn… something. We saw each other for a while, then he moved on, and then at some point I saw him again and I think he said he had a kid…"

Bracken gaped at her. "You dated Sean's father?"

"Shh—" Jaz shoved the photos in her back pocket and moved to the espresso machine. "He's coming."

"You don't know the potential gold mine you have down there," Sean said as he approached the counter. "You have enough stuff to fill a museum. Probably make a nice profit from something like that too."

Jaz found a rag and rubbed it across the espresso machine. "I already have to run one business. I'm not interested in starting another. Besides, I don't want more people in here."

"You don't?"

"No. I want to be left alone."

Sean watched her over the top of espresso machine. "I don't believe that."

Jaz glanced up at him, then away. "What do you know?"

Sean shrugged. "I know I want to see that coffee roaster before I go. It's vintage."

Jaz hesitated, then nodded. "Come on."

They went downstairs and Jaz turned on a hanging light bulb above the roaster. It was a large machine, wider than it was tall, with a rectangular furnace attached to a wide round drum where the beans were roasted. Burlap sacks of unroasted beans were piled on short shelves nearby. The roasted beans were kept on shelves closer to the basement stairs where they were more easily accessible.

Sean passed a hand over the side of the roaster. "I've never seen one like this before."

"It's an old model."

"You keep it in good condition."

Jaz tipped her head to one side, watching him. "You know something about roasters?"

"My dad was a mechanic. He would take apart old machines and restore them. Mostly washers and toaster ovens. He had a few coffee-related machines come through his workshop. He built a roaster out of a steel drum and a heat gun."

Jaz smiled. "He sounds like a smart guy."

"He was. He passed away a few years ago."

"I'm sorry." Jaz touched the photo in her back pocket, trying to think of something to say. "Did he teach you about roasting?"

"Yeah. He loved good coffee, and now so do I. An unfortunate side effect of course is most others taste like dirt to me. I can't go anywhere and just enjoy a cup of coffee because it's coffee. I have to have the best." He looked at her and smiled, more with his eyes than his mouth this time.

Jaz smirked. "I don't see the problem."

He smirked back, then after a moment said, "So… Bracken tells me you're related."

"Yeah. He ran into some trouble and I'm helping him out."

"What kind of trouble?"

"Just… family stuff."

Sean made a dismissive gesture. "It's all right. Not my business."

"I can't talk about it." She shrugged apologetically.

Sean sighed, looking down at the empty drum of the roaster. "Thing is, I'd like to see you again."

"You will when you stop by after the next heist."

"I meant, maybe for lunch sometime."

"I…"

"I'll need a couple of days to get the gang squared away and the spoils divvied up, and then we can…" He took a short breath. "You're going to say no though."

Jaz had stopped breathing, her eyes avoiding him. "I can't leave the shop. I'm the only one running it."

"What about Bracken?"

"He's been here three days. He doesn't know anything. I'm sorry. I just can't leave."

"How long have you been here?"

"A few years."

"No one collects that much junk in just a few years unless they're actively stealing it."

"I'm a kleptomaniac."

Sean raised his eyebrows at her.

Jaz looked down shuffled her feet. "We can have lunch here, if you still want to."

Sean nodded slowly, rubbing his jaw. He moved toward the stairs as if to pass her but stopped just before he did. His head and shoulders were a few inches above her own. He looked down at her and said quietly, "Whatever's going on with you, with this place, you don't have to tell me. But you don't need to lie either."

Jaz took a slow breath. "If you want to talk coffee, tell me about yourself, fine. I can't... I'm not ready to talk about myself just yet."

"Fair enough. We'll talk coffee until you're ready. And here. Just in case you change your mind." He handed her a slip of paper, smiled, and went upstairs.

Jaz stayed where she was for a moment, looking at the paper. Then she followed Sean upstairs. He was by the doors when she emerged from the basement, surrounded by his posse.

He smiled at her, waved to Bracken, and went out the doors for the last time. The last strains of music from the hi-fi, carried under J.P.'s arm, lingered in the shop a moment, then faded away.

Jaz crossed the room and locked the doors, then turned the sign in the window to 'closed.'

As soon as the thieves had gone, Bracken dropped the napkins he was holding and waded through the mess of cups on the floor of the workspace to join Jaz. "Did you tell him? What did he say?"

Jaz made a face and turned away from the doors. "No, I didn't tell him. That would have been weird. Especially after he gave me his number."

"Wha— really? But you dated his father."

"A long time ago," said Jaz, slipping the paper into her vest pocket. "So what?"

"It's just, weird. What if he turned out to be… you know…"

Jaz raised an eyebrow.

"Your son, or something."

She snorted, shouldering past him to the counter. "Don't be an idiot. I can't have children."

"You can't?"

She spun toward him, flinging out her arms. "Think about it. What happens at midnight?"

"The shop resets… oh."

"And I'm part of the shop. I reset too. Back to how I was on day one."

"Right." Bracken glanced down, feeling a little silly. "I guess… you've outlived a lot of boyfriends."

Jaz looked at him a moment, her face still. "Yeah. I guess I have."

"What about Athamas?" Bracken sat down on a stool and rested his arms on the countertop. The shop was far from organized, but Bracken felt he deserved a break.

Jaz took a stool beside him. "What about him?"

"He's Tuoni, right?"

"Tuoni?"

"The carrier of souls, to the afterlife."

"Different worlds give him different names. Hel, Vanth, Arawn, Nephthys. In Grayson's Gulch he's one of the seven fates. I just call him Athamas." Jaz stood and went around the counter to the pastry case, ignoring sleeves of cups rocking gently in her wake, and pulled out a tin of blueberry cobbler.

"Is that his real name?"

"It's what Corrine calls him." Jaz returned to her stool beside Bracken and scooped some cobbler out with a spoon.

"The girl who was with him? Who's she?"

"I'm not sure." Jaz swallowed the cobbler and grimaced, touching her bruised throat with her fingertips. "She follows him around, being sarcastic mostly. I've never seen her interact with someone who is dying. Only Athamas does. His job seems to be guiding souls from life to what comes after. I think Corrine handles them after they've crossed over, or whatever."

Bracken nodded, his chin resting on his forearms. Now that he was sitting, his fatigue was almost overwhelming. Jaz set a plate and fork beside his elbow and dished out a generous helping of cobbler. Bracken eyed it tiredly. He was hungry, but not for more syrupy, sugary pastry. His middle gurgled, so he took a few bites to appease it.

Jaz was still talking about Athamas, and the day they met. "He was so angry I was still alive. Like I was cheating him out of his last meal or something. He kept pointing to this notebook he keeps with him, saying, 'you're supposed to be dead! Now my ledger won't balance.' And Corrine pesters him about keeping analog records, but he's old school and stubborn — anyway, after he calmed down, he decided he'll figure out a way to make me die, eventually. In the meantime he stops in for coffee and cobbler when he's not busy…"

Bracken laid the fork down and nudged the plate away. Part of him, the ever-curious part, wanted to ask if Athamas had taken Sadie when she — but the other part of him, the raw, reactive part that still couldn't accept Sadie was actually gone, shut the question down instantly. He didn't want to know. Not when there was a chance Sadie could still be found in another of these worlds — namely, Saturday.

The next day.

Bracken excused himself and went to his room. He meant to study Saturday's binder again, to plan as much as possible. He stared at pictures of Davin, memorizing the young man's face. According to the binder, Davin and his friends often studied at The Defiant. There was no guarantee Davin would show up, of course, but that didn't matter. Even if he didn't show up, it just gave Bracken more time to plan until the next week. The great thing about this coffee shop was that it was on a loop. He had infinite opportunities to find his aunt. He would have to get Davin to help him locate Sadie, and then find a way to bring her to the shop...

His dreams that night were all about seeing her again.

31

Introduction to Alchemy

Jaz pulled Bracken out of bed the next morning at sunrise. "You need to come see this."

Bracken sat up slowly. His limbs felt like they'd been replaced with wood. For a moment he couldn't remember where he was. "Don't wanna… tired…"

He vaguely recalled falling asleep with Saturday's binder on his lap. It was now facedown on the floor.

Jaz, who didn't seem to share his exhaustion, gathered the binder and the loose pictures that had fallen from it, took him by the arm and towed him out of the room and up the stairs. Her Friday melancholy had vanished: now she was all upbeat. "Sleep when you get home. You'll only see this once." She deposited him on a stool, splashed some coffee into a mug and set it in front of him.

Bracken sipped between sluggish blinks. The windows showed only a gray-yellow pallor with hazy smudges visible in the distance. "What day is it now?"

"Saturday." Jaz filled a plate with muffins and set it in front of Bracken.

Bracken gave the plate a tired look and sipped again. His head felt light, threatening to detach and float away. "Why are we up so early?"

"Watch." Jaz pointed at the windows.

Bracken turned reluctantly, rubbing his eyes and blinking until they remembered how to focus.

It was growing light outside. Bracken could see The Defiant was perched on a terraced hill, in line with a curved row of quaint shops, all attached to each other. The street out front was a smooth flow of red brickwork. Directly in front of the windows, a solid circle of white bricks marked a circular patio bulging outward, over the terrace.

Bracken squinted. "Nice patio. Do you put out chairs?"

"I can't go outside," Jaz reminded him, "and it's not a patio."

"What is it?"

"That, is an airship landing pad."

Beyond and below the landing pad, a city of brick and stone spread out like the top of a footprint, surrounded by mountains on three sides. Streets and alleyways lit by naked golden flames traced a bright maze around the buildings. Many buildings had flat rooftops, with narrow stone walkways arching from roof to roof. Yellow vapor trails grew from a forest of narrow chimneys, and clouds billowed from smokestacks of the larger fortresses. The smoke joined into a dull yellow supercloud coating the sky.

A cluster of buildings stood tall in the center of the city, all white granite, their square rooftops connected by walkways converging like a spider web above a sprawling courtyard.

"That's the Academy of Alchemy." Jaz pointed at these buildings.

Bracken bit into a muffin and said through the mouthful, "Alchemy? Like magic?" He had been wondering about this while he studied the pictures from Saturday's binder.

"In Vasencea it's what they call manipulating the elements. Some people here are born with the ability, and they spend years in training, learning to master it." She pointed to the south. "That building is the robotics factory. They make giant mechanical suits of armor, basically. And that castle with the pointy towers is the Capitol building. Vasencea is the capitol of the Northern Province."

"Okay." Bracken sipped away at the coffee, as if drinking faster might weigh him down while lightening his eyelids.

Then suddenly they felt much lighter. A large group of people in light blue tunics had just emerged from stairwells set in the rooftops. These people were followed by a second group dressed in amber robes. The Tunics lined up on the walkways between the roofs, while the Robes formed circles on the roofs and did some kind of choreography, waving their arms gracefully like orchestra conductors.

It was mesmerizing.

"What are they doing?" Bracken asked, not taking his eyes from the performance.

"Just watch."

The tiny oval flames lining the streets flashed from gold to bright blue, and rose above the rooftops, guided by the robed conductors. When the flames reached the level of the walkways, they suddenly extinguished. The Tunics spread their arms and fell forward. For a moment they plummeted toward the streets, stroking their arms like swimmers, and then they soared upward, carving graceful curves with their bodies. They shot up past the rooftops, toward the thick yellow cloud. They swirled against the hazy backdrop for a moment, turning arbitrarily, lazily, and then suddenly formed two lines facing each other high over the middle of the city. The lines swept toward each other and crossed, picking up speed. The clouds split behind the lines like parting curtains, revealing a widening stripe of ice-blue sky. White bars of sunlight struck into the city, evaporating the last curls of fog: the sun was already shining above the mountains.

The two flying lines swept the halves of the yellow cloud north and south, pushing them along until they gained their own momentum and sailed away, out of sight.

Bracken saluted the spectacle with his coffee cup, sloshing some over the rim. "They do that every morning?"

"Yeah. It's a ritual. They have to clear away the vapors made by the smokestacks. The sky will stay mostly clear until evening."

"Why don't they just shut off the chimneys?"

"Can't. Those vapors power the city." Jaz cleared away the remains of their breakfast, dumping cobbler into the garbage and dropping the plates carelessly in the dishwasher.

Bracken finished his coffee and slid the empty mug toward her. "Why don't they find a way to power the city without choking up the sky?"

"It's not easy to change that. Their whole infrastructure relies on steam power. They use alchemy to convert water instantly to steam. The steam heats their homes, powers their airships, all machinery… They use it for everything. Except drinking, ironically. Water is strictly rationed. I have a permit to prove I've got a water ration, even though the shop doesn't use water from Vasencea."

The idea of The Defiant being self-supplied was interesting, but now was not the time to get sidetracked. They were only in Vasencea for a day. "Are they running out of water?"

"Yes. They can turn it into vapors but not the other way round." Jaz went to the back counter and scanned the bags of coffee beans sitting in a long line, three rows deep.

"Whoever invented steam power must be kicking themselves," Bracken observed.

"You would think so." Jaz shrugged, looking at dates written sloppily in marker on the bags of beans. She selected four bags and stowed them beneath a shelf near the espresso machine. "They use alchemy to grow plants composed of mostly water. They harvest the moisture from the plants and ship it to the cities to power them."

"They manufacture water so they can keep turning it into yellow fog."

Jaz picked up the chalkboard by the register and wrote down the coffee of the day. "Hey, you celebrate Cabbage Week. Every world has its quirks."

Bracken's reply was cut off by a deep yawn. "…next time I'm going to be sure to sleep every night. This is brutal," he said, when he could talk again.

Jaz stopped writing, her face suddenly still. "Bracken… there can't be a next time. On Monday you're going home with your sister."

Bracken blinked. "Come on, Jaz. You don't expect me to go home after all this." He swung an open hand toward the city beyond the windows.

"You have to. You have a family out there, and a life to live. You need to go back to them."

"I could have a life here. Like Sadie did."

Jaz shook her head. "This isn't living. This is… perpetual existence."

He leaned forward on his stool. "What about the doorway generator, and getting you out of here?"

"It was never going to happen. And I'm not going to let you waste your life here. She wouldn't want you to either."

"I think she would. And I don't think she'd appreciate you calling her life a waste."

Jaz's eyes snapped up to his. "Hey. I didn't mean it like that."

"I know you didn't. But even so. You could use some help here anyway…" Bracken trailed off as he noticed a large shape descending on the landing pad outside. He stared for a moment, then said slowly, "A… giant barrel just landed outside."

Jaz set the chalkboard beside the register. "It's an airship. If you go closer to the windows you can see the rest of it."

Bracken stood, chin raised, and walked into the workspace, stopping behind the register. "I can't right now. I'm on register."

Jaz raised an eyebrow. "Now you're willing to work."

"Unless you want me to make the coffee."

Jaz moved quickly to take her spot by the espresso machine. "This conversation isn't over," she muttered as the doors opened and customers approached the counter.

"I'm just getting started," he muttered back, then grinned and raised his voice. "Hello! Welcome to The Defiant. What can we make you?"

32

Cappuccino Nazi

The morning passed in a rush. Airships landed every hour on the hour, their huge bellies touching down on the landing pad, letting down stairs from rectangular hatches stretching accordion-like to the bricks.

Passengers disembarked and flowed into The Defiant, while waiting customers rushed out the doors to catch the next departure. In these crowds were women in flowing skirts and patent leather walking boots, clean-shaven men with trim sideburns wearing smart suits and lacy cravats, carrying leather satchels smelling of lavender and money; officers in dark blue uniforms, their shining boots squeaking on the floor tiles.

Mixed in among them were young people from the Academy of Alchemy, wearing jackets and blazers with patches affixed to the shoulder, toting satchels bulging with textbooks.

The shop swelled full of bodies and luggage, emptied and swelled again. The Defiant began to seem more like a train station than a coffee shop.

A line of customers pressed toward the counter, shuffling satchels and suitcases, checking their pocket watches. Bracken scrawled a list of drink orders on a miniature chalkboard stationed near the espresso machine for Jaz, who was churning out about ninety drinks per minute. The line continued to build. As Bracken waded through the onslaught of orders, ringing up customers and trying to make correct change out of unfamiliar currency, Jaz zoomed around the workspace, making drinks and picking up his slack.

"Bracken I need you to prep the cups before you give them to me."

"...right. Sorry."

"Refill that hopper before it's empty. Where are those cups?"

"Oh... yeah. Um..." He turned slowly in a circle, overwhelmed by the multitude of tasks.

"Never mind." Jaz seemed to be making five different types of drinks at once. "Go finish those pourovers."

Bracken gave the waiting pourover vessels a tired look. He ground beans and poured water on them at intervals while customers in line watched impatiently. His body felt sluggish and heavy, but he refused Jaz the satisfaction of showing his fatigue. If she kicked him out of The Defiant, he would never find Sadie. He had begun to think of the alternate Sadie as his aunt, regardless of what Jaz said. Any version of Sadie was better than none at all. So he stood straight and took drink orders and worked the register as if he had been born to do nothing else.

Outside, the belly of another airship touched down on the landing pad. Hinges squealed faintly. Yellow vapors hissed out of the engines and curled against The Defiant's windows. People filed into the shop in a line that seemed unending. But then suddenly, the last customer was walking out with their drink, marking the end of that rush. The shop was nearly empty for a few minutes, save for a handful of young people huddled over textbooks at various tables, until the next airship brought a new crowd.

Jaz pulled espresso into two demitasse cups and set one next to Bracken. "Tired?"

He shook his head no. They drank the shots, Bracken tossing his back with a wince and Jaz swallowing hers with a thoughtful look. She rinsed the shot glasses and dropped them into the dishwasher. "The rushes are predictable, at least."

Bracken rested against the counter, resisting the urge to slump over it. "How do you do this by yourself?"

"I'm very efficient." She looked at a young man sitting alone at the counter. "By yourself today, Davin?"

Bracken stiffened, snapping his head around to look at the young man. In all the flurry and hustle, he hadn't even noticed him there. His surprise was quickly replaced with irritation at himself. How long had Davin been sitting there, while he was occupied pouring coffees and counting change? Irritation was just as quickly replaced by excitement. Davin was here, and Bracken was one step closer to finally finding his aunt.

Davin looked up at Jaz. His brown hair was a little longer and his large, brown eyes were a little older than in the photos. "I wish. Costello is meeting me here in a few minutes. Exams are next week."

"Right." Jaz pulled another shot and set it in front of him with a small glass of sparkling water. "Here. On the house."

"Thanks." Davin's smile brightened his pale face considerably. His cheeks were rounded, sprinkled with freckles. He wore a light blue jacket, zipped partway up. The high collar was folded down, wide lapels almost reaching his shoulders.

Jaz knocked the spent puck of espresso grounds from the portafilter with more force than necessary. "If you happen to spill it on him when he gets here it's all right with me."

Davin took a stack of books from the backpack sitting on the counter in front of him. "It's okay, Jaz."

"Sure…" Jaz shook her head.

Bracken, who had been staring at Davin and growing more and more electrified, finally found his voice. He pointed suddenly at Davin. "I have that jacket. Had it. I used to have that jacket!"

Davin blinked at him.

"Weigh out more beans for pourovers while we have time, Bracken," said Jaz, a little louder than necessary.

Bracken ignored her. "Where does it come from? I mean, where did you get it?"

"They're part of our uniform." Davin turned to show a patch on his right shoulder.

It read 'Vasencea Academy of Alchemy' across the top and 'Primovera' across the bottom. A brown bird with wings spread in flight was embroidered in the center of the patch.

Bracken leaned toward him over the counter, grinning. "I knew it! You're him!"

Davin leaned back. "Pardon?"

"Davin who doesn't believe in rainbows!"

"…what?"

"Battle stations, Bracken." Jaz pushed him toward the register. The front runners of the next rush were stepping through the door.

Bracken skipped backwards with outstretched arms. "Sadie! You knew my aunt!"

Davin's mouth dropped open.

Giggling under his breath, Bracken turned to the first waiting customer, a stately young woman wearing a neat blue blazer with an Academy patch on the shoulder. Her long golden hair was twisted into a loose knot at the base of her head.

"What flavors do you have?" she asked.

"Vanilla!" He cheered.

"Do you have anything else?" She had a sharp, intelligent look that grew sharper as she narrowed her eyes in scrutiny.

"Nope!" Bracken said brightly, drumming his fingers on the edge of the counter and glancing at Davin, who was staring at him in shock.

"Yes you do." The young lady gestured at the row of syrup bottles near the espresso machine. "I can see them right there."

"I bet I know which one you want though."

"The point is you said you didn't have anything else when in fact you do," she said, in a show of being patient.

Bracken shrugged. "You're right. Sorry. Which flavor do you want?"

"An iced vanilla cappuccino please," she said coldly.

"You got it!" He slapped the syrup into a pint glass and set it by the espresso machine.

"Iced vanilla cappuccino," he announced to Jaz.

Jaz picked up the cup and looked at it with disgust, as if it were a particularly ugly slug that had crawled up from the drain. Directing her disgust at the young woman, she said, "We've been through this, Clara. An iced cappuccino is not a thing."

"I assure you it is," said Clara, her cheeks reddening.

"It's physically impossible," Jaz retorted. "You do not get foam in an iced drink. Whipped cream — fine. If I served it. Which I don't. Foam — forget it. And I'm not spooning foam over the top of the damn thing. That's just ridiculous."

Clara set her jaw, sighing through closed teeth. "It is neither ridiculous nor impossible. I've had it here before."

"You're getting an iced latte. That's what you're getting."

Bracken felt this argument was wasting precious time. He edged over to Jaz. "Couldn't you just make it for her this once?"

Jaz removed a portafilter from the espresso machine and thrust it toward Bracken's chest. "Absolutely not."

"Why not?"

"Because I am the immortal goddess of coffee and I refuse!" Jaz snarled, wagging the portafilter for emphasis.

"Fine…" Clara made an impatient gesture with one hand. "I don't know how you stay in business."

"I don't know why you keep coming back." Jaz hefted the glass in her other hand, seeming to consider hurling it at the young woman, but instead set it down so hard it rang.

Bracken turned away from Jaz as she began pulling shots, unsure whether to laugh at her or shake her. Any other time, he would have found this whole exchange quite funny. But he was running out of time and Jaz seemed determined to make it impossible for him to talk to Davin.

"Incorrigible," Clara muttered, making her way to Davin.

He leaned slightly away as she sat on a stool beside him.

"Hello Davin." She smiled, her face becoming quite pretty. "Waiting for Costello?"

"Yes," Davin muttered, looking down at his books.

"I just saw him on the road as we landed. He'll be here any minute."

"I know."

A tiny frown puckered Clara's forehead for a moment. "Ah, I forgot your ability. You must have seen me coming also."

Davin shrugged and nodded, avoiding her eyes.

Bracken sidled close to Jaz with a questioning look

"He sees what the wind sees — it's Alchemy stuff. They call it Farsight." Jaz muttered back. She set Clara's drink before her on the counter. "Are you and Costello still dating? Why don't you take him for a nice romantic walk when he gets here? Davin doesn't need his help."

A larger frown creased Clara's brow and her mouth tightened. "I think Costello is being very nice to help Davin study. The entrance exam for the Flier program is quite difficult."

"That blighter doesn't help people. He uses them," said Jaz.

Clara straightened on her stool, preparing a rebuttal.

"It's all right, Jaz," said Davin quickly. He gathered his books and slid from his stool.

Clara smiled at him in a matronly way, then stood also. "I was going to meet him, but the atmosphere here is too disagreeable. Let him know I said hello, will you, Davin?"

Davin nodded vaguely. Clara flounced out of the shop, leaving her unpaid-for drink on the counter. Jaz left it there and returned to her spot at the espresso machine, muttering rude-sounding words in a language Bracken didn't recognize.

"My name is Bracken, by the way, " Bracken said to Davin, watching Jaz from the corner of his eye. "I'm staying with Jaz for a while."

Davin looked up, meeting Bracken's eyes for the first time. "Nice to meet you. Sadie mentioned she had a nephew."

Bracken nodded, feeling more lightheaded than before. "I saw — I mean, she told me about you too. She liked you."

Davin's cheeks and neck flushed pink, and he looked down at his hands. "She's a good friend. I haven't heard from her since she got sick. How is she doing?"

"Sick? Ah…" Bracken blinked. He looked at Jaz, who shook her head at him, swiping a damp towel over the counter, sending crumbs flying. His mind spun into high gear as he realized Jaz hadn't told Davin the truth either. Which was actually good news for Bracken. "Yeah. Yeah… she's… doing better now. She's… living… out in the country with family, I think. How long did… have you known her?"

"Since I came to Vasencea from the country for basic training. She got sick a few months ago, just after I graduated and started at the Academy. I gave her one of my jackets. I'm glad to hear she's doing better. Missed seeing her here…" His voice trailed to a whisper and he glanced furtively at the doors as they opened and Costello swaggered in.

33

Dual Intentions

If anyone had been formed and intended by nature to be a pirate, it was this young man. Broad shouldered, barrel chested, with a jaw that seemed about to sprout a seaman's beard any moment, Costello strode into The Defiant like a captain taking command of a ship. Davin retreated to an empty table, away from the counter.

"The usual, Jaz!" Costello bellowed, waving in her direction. Heads turned toward him. He accepted the reaction as natural and continued to the next point of order. He found Davin with a sweeping glance and strode to him, smoothly stepping around suitcases and handbags as if they weren't there.

"So!" Costello sat across from Davin. "Did you get the hang of the cyclone yet?"

Davin reply was too quiet to hear as he pressed into the back of his chair, possibly in hopes it might absorb him.

Jaz stood at the espresso machine, needlessly swirling a towel inside a clean portafilter, eyes bulging with thoughts of violence.

Bracken, standing beside her, asked incredulously, "That guy is helping Davin?"

Jaz shook her head. "He's supposedly 'helping' Davin learn advanced Alchemy techniques. As if Davin needed it. He's incredibly gifted. His Farsight ability alone could get him promoted to the top of any career he chooses. He wants to get into the Fliers, and unfortunately so does Costello. He's making Davin take the entrance exam for him. If he doesn't, Costello will get him expelled."

"How?"

"Money. He's rich and his family has influence. That's all it takes to get what you want here. He'd buy his way into the program but the Captain who runs it makes everyone pass a written exam. No exceptions. She's one of the only officers in Vasencea who's not completely corrupt."

"So since Costello can't buy his way in, he'll just cheat."

"Yep. And Davin thinks he can't refuse because Costello is high in the pecking order."

"We can't let him get away with that."

"What do you want me to do? Knock him out and throw him in the basement?" Jaz refilled her espresso grinder from a bag of beans beneath the counter. "It's their business, not ours. You can't go trying to fix whatever's wrong in these worlds. It'll just drive you insane. And what do you care anyway? You're not going to see any of them again."

Bracken watched her, trembling with sudden anger. "I don't know why anyone still comes in this shop, the way you treat them."

Jaz glanced briefly back at him. "If you're not going to work, get out of my way. There's another rush starting."

Bracken turned and marched out, pounding downstairs and into his room. He grabbed Sadie's picture from among the others scattered over his bed, stared at it a moment, then pulled off his shirt and shed his pants. He set his jaw and marched back upstairs, changing shape on the way. Halfway up, his chest and hips were effeminately curved, legs joining into a long, elegant skirt. Three-quarters up, his torso was a smart blue blazer with wide lapels and a Vasencea patch. At the top, he paused to adjust the lapels of the jacket and pat the golden hair twisted into a smart bun at the base of his head.

He paused again at the top of the stairs, resting a shaking hand on the door. He had never been so angry before. It was a shock how quickly his temper had flared up. He didn't even know he'd had one before this. Possibly, lack of sleep and a constant diet of pastries over the past few days had something to do with it. Bracken shook his head and breathed deeply, forcing his hands to steady. Davin could help him find Sadie. Costello was getting in the way.

And if Jaz had *her* way, this was the first and only chance Bracken would have with Davin. He didn't know what he'd do once he enlisted Davin's help, but that didn't matter as much as getting to Davin in the first place.

He emerged from the basement transformed into a tall, graceful female human. He crossed the room, weaving around customers and their luggage until he reached the table where Costello sat with Davin.

"There you are, dear," Bracken said, bending his voice to a female tone and laying a hand on Costello's shoulder. "I need to talk to you."

Davin was just sliding a stack of papers across the table to Costello. He froze, staring up at Bracken.

Costello twisted around. "Clara! I didn't know you were here."

Davin tried to hide the papers beneath the table, but Bracken quickly leaned down and snatched them up. Costello stood just as quickly and grabbed Bracken's slender, white wrist. "That's just Davin's homework. We're not quite finished yet…"

Bracken gave Costello an imperious look and pulled free. He scanned the top sheet, frowning. It was filled with shaky writing, with a lot of diagrams and formulas. Bracken glimpsed a few words like 'swiftness' and 'whirlwind vector', but didn't understand any of it. Fortunately, he didn't need to. "Are these test answers?"

Costello moved uneasily at Bracken's side. "It's not what it looks like—"

"It looks like you're making this young man cheat for you," Bracken said loudly, putting as much cold disdain as he could manage into his voice. It wasn't very difficult. Clara's way of speaking was a lot like Jaz's, but with less profanity.

"No, it's not like that—" Costello tried to lower his voice, and managed to get it to a near rumble. He put a thick arm around Bracken's waist and walked him toward the doors, away from the watching eyes of customers — many of them fellow students. "I'm trying to help the kid but he's so bad at alchemy… it's a lot of work, but what am I supposed to do, send him away?"

Costello was beginning to sound like Jaz, which made Bracken's anger surge up again. He pulled sharply away.

"Davin has more ability than you do! He has foresight—"

"Farsight—"

"And he's a good person, and he's smart enough, and he doesn't need your help! He worked his way here on his own, without any money or relatives—"

"Clara—"

"And he doesn't need you, or Jaz, or anyone else! He can find her without you, and you know what — you need *him!*"

Costello had let go of Bracken's arm, and was looking more confused than ever. "What are you talking about? Find who?"

"Costello, what's going on?"

Bracken shut his mouth with a snap. Clara — the real Clara — was standing behind him in the doorway. She came to stand by Costello and gasped, putting a hand to her mouth as she saw Clara-Bracken.

Costello stared from one Clara to the other, open-mouthed. Then he recovered himself and grabbed Bracken's arm again, this time clamping down hard and growling, "Who are you?"

Bracken smiled weakly, curtsied, and shrank the arm Costello was holding, slipping out of his grasp. Costello grabbed for him again, but Bracken dodged away, skipping back toward Davin's table. "Everyone knows now what you've been doing! You can't make Davin cheat for you anymore! If you want to get at him, go through *me* first!"

Bracken flounced to a stop in front of Davin's table and grinned at him. Davin looked both awed and incredulous. Jaz had stopped working and was staring at Bracken, her expression a mixture of horror and disbelief.

Everyone in the café was still and staring. The room held a collective breath. Then everyone was pushing back chairs, grabbing luggage, and hurrying for the doors.

Davin stood too, but stayed at the table, facing Bracken. "Are you sure about this…?"

"About what?" Bracken turned to look back.

"The duel. The one you just challenged him to?"

At the same time, Jaz shouted from behind the counter: "He didn't mean it—! Bracken get down!"

Costello swept his hands together, lacing his fingers into one fist, and punched them toward Bracken. He was standing too far away to touch Bracken, and for a moment Bracken thought it was only a gesture. The next instant, an invisible force punched Bracken's stomach so hard he felt it go through him. He fell backward, then rolled onto his side, curling his knees to his chest. A dull pain settled and expanded in his middle, as if he had swallowed a large rock. A hot wetness trickled down his stomach. He couldn't breathe. Faintly, he heard Jaz yelling, and hollow thumping, but all sounds and sights were made fuzzy by the pain and the sudden ringing in his ears.

34

Pitcher This

"You get out!" Jaz grabbed the nearest thing to hand, a half-full jug of milk, and hurled it at Costello. "No fighting in my shop!"

He had been taken by surprise at Bracken's sudden defeat, and ducked too late. The jug hit him in the chest, and he staggered back, nearly falling.

Costello straightened, only to dodge another milk jug — this one was full — and then a syrup bottle, which smashed against an overturned table. Next came a heavy portafilter, which shot past his head and cracked a window.

Costello stumbled backward, guarding his face with raised arms as Jaz continued to launch things at him as she moved along the counter toward the register and her shotgun beneath it. She had finished with the syrup bottles and moved on to silver steaming pitchers. The pitchers pinged brightly, some hitting him and some sailing past, bouncing and skipping across the floor.

Clara strode into the line of fire, teeth clenched, hands balled in fists alongside her swishing skirt. Placing herself between Costello and Jaz, she made wide circular gestures with both hands. Sudden gusts of wind rose around her and sent the pitchers spinning off to either side. The wind swirled her skirts and tugged brown wisps of hair from her bun so they floated around her face like seaweed in water.

Jaz reached for another pitcher, but she had run out. She grabbed the shotgun and pumped it, but it was empty. So she threw it instead. "Get out of my shop! Get out!"

Clara continued making her circular gestures to maintain the gusts for a moment, in case Jaz found something else to throw, but Jaz was done and so Clara lowered her hands and the wind died away.

Jaz vaulted over the counter, crunching shards of glass beneath her boots as she landed on the other side, and dashed over to Bracken. She slipped in something wet as she neared him and crashed to her knees. The wetness was a warm pool around Bracken, soaking her pant legs. Jaz didn't look down to see if it was blood or spilled coffee. Davin had knelt beside him already, crouched with one hand pressed against Bracken's back, staring intently at his chest. A small hole had opened up, leaking pale pink blood.

Jaz put her hands on Bracken's shoulders and looked into his face with rising panic. "Bracken. Bracken!"

Bracken raised his head. His eyes were solid black behind his fluttering eyelids. He wheezed a sound but couldn't draw breath back in. His body trembled. His clothes, which were really just his skin, were losing shape and color. He raised shaking hands and clutched at her shoulders.

Davin pushed Jaz away and made a pulling, twisting gesture in front of Bracken's chest with one hand, as if drawing out an invisible string. His other hand pressed firmly against the middle of Bracken's quivering back.

The rocklike pain in Bracken's chest seemed to bulge, then stretch, and then it tunneled out of him toward Davin's moving hand. Bracken spasmed as the thing left him — and suddenly he could breathe again. He gulped air. Jaz leaned in and pulled him against her, wrapping her arms around him while looking over his shoulder to Davin.

Davin told her, "It was trapped inside him. It's all out now. We should get some bandages and stop the bleeding."

"What was it?" Bracken asked hoarsely.

"Air," said Davin.

"Oh," said Bracken, and passed out.

35

Fast Forward

Moving him only made the bleeding worse so they left him on the floor. Jaz ran to the kitchen and found a pile of bar towels to tuck under his head.

Davin nudged a suitcase under Bracken's legs to elevate them. "There are medics nearby. I'll go and bring one."

Jaz cradled Bracken's head. He seemed smaller than usual, as if all his mass was draining out of him. Medicine wouldn't help him, she was certain, nor Alchemy. Nothing would. "Sure, yes. Go. Get them."

Davin hurried out. Jaz waited until the doors closed behind him, then laid Bracken's head gently on the floor. She ran across the empty café — Clara and Costello had gone, at some point, along with everyone else — locked the doors, and raced back to Bracken. He looked worse than ever, his body too thin and flaccid as she pulled his head and shoulders into her lap.

"Janus!" She cried, her voice rising to a scream. "Janus!!"

Janus appeared, sitting on a nearby suitcase. "That doesn't look good."

"Shut up! You have to help him."

Janus crossed one knee over the other. "The wound is beyond healing, you realize. To save his life I would have to — "

"I know!"

"I can't use such power on him. Not without his permission."

"You have mine, now do it!"

Janus uncrossed his knees and leaned forward. A sharp expression came into his face. "If I do this for you, I'll want something in return."

"You always do, don't you? You can't save a life just because it's a life, can you?" Jaz clutched Bracken to her, his arms and head falling limply over her arms.

Janus shook his head. "It doesn't affect me who dies or lives in these worlds. You want his life to continue, not me."

"What then?" she hissed, clenching her teeth against a sharp sob. "What do you want?"

"I want you to let me approach him without interfering. Or trying to dissuade him from making an agreement of his own with me."

"So his life only matters if it benefits you," Jaz growled.

"Fortunately for you, yes." Janus stood, shimmering with

waves of iridescence traveling down his body into the floor. "Do we have an agreement then?"

Jaz looked down at Bracken. "Yes. We have an agreement. Dammit."

Janus nodded. He turned and looked up at the ceiling, a slight smile lifting the corners of his mouth. "Athamas isn't going to like this…"

Iridescent ripples shot across the floor, up the walls, coating everything in the shop.

Then the shaking began: a violent, deep tremor hanging in the air like discordant base notes, flooding and pounding through every inch of the room.

Jaz curled over Bracken, hugging him to her. "It'll be okay… just hold on a second longer. One more second…"

And then the shrieking began, like the sound of wheels on metal, and a slick, rushing sound like a record played at high speed.

The hands of the clock above the doors accelerated. The second hand spun too fast to be seen, while the hour hand advanced smoothly, passing the hours until they both stopped at midnight.

36

The Last Present

Bracken woke in darkness on his back, wet, and alone. He sat up and winced, putting a hand to his chest. It ached dully, like a deep bruise. He went to call out for Jaz, but coughed instead.

Footsteps pounded up the stairs and someone burst through the basement door. Bracken heard heavy thumpings and chairs skidding across the floor, then Jaz was hugging him tightly.

He winced, letting his arms hang at his sides. His chin rested on her shoulder. "Did I die?"

"Almost. You healed when the shop reset." Jaz released him and sat back against a tall suitcase, half-closing her eyes. A bit of silver light from a full moon shone through the windows, so pale and colorless Bracken couldn't tell if Jaz's skin was unusually white or just painted with moonlight.

He wondered vaguely about the suitcase. Suitcas*es*, he realized as his eyes adjusted to the semi-darkness, and an array of luggage around the room became somewhat visible. "What happened?"

"You don't remember?" Jaz moved her eyes toward him. "You challenged Costello to a duel and he shot you."

That triggered a memory. Bracken flinched and felt his chest again. "With… air."

"Yeah." Jaz narrowed her stare into a glare. "What were you thinking? That was absolutely the stupidest thing you've done yet."

"I didn't know he'd try to kill me—"

"He wasn't trying to. It was a basic strike, about as forceful as a hard punch to humans."

Bracken shook his head. "That was more than just a punch."

"Yeah, because you're not a human. I keep telling you, stay out of trouble, but you just had to go and—"

Bracken sat up on his knees. "You never said stay out of trouble."

Jaz thumped her forehead with the heels of both hands. "It was implied! You've seen what can happen here — I died for fates' sake! Twice, almost." She thrust her hands toward him. "What in *hells* is wrong with you?"

"I just wanted to find Sadie. You wouldn't help, so…"

"You can't find Sadie! She's gone, okay? She's dead."

The bruised, aching place in Bracken's chest tightened.

"But I can find her. Davin could have found her alternate," Bracken muttered, suddenly struggling to speak past the ache.

Jaz surged forward on her knees, splashing through a puddle of thin liquid on the floor, stirring up a pungent smell. She grabbed his shoulders. "Stop it, Bracken! You can't bring her back by latching onto someone who looks like her! Sadie is gone. And I'm sorry. I'm really sorry. But she's gone."

The tight ache moved into Bracken's throat, making him unable to speak. He watched Jaz's face, which was near expressionless. She turned her head, like she always did when a conversation got too personal. Except this time he felt trembling emotion in her fingers like electricity.

"It's my fault," Jaz continued softly, tears gathering in her eyes. "I should have sent her away. I just… couldn't."

Seeing her this way loosed something in his throat, and he could speak again. "She stayed because she didn't want to be with us. My family — we chased her away. My dad especially. He hated that she traveled. He would argue with her every time she visited, tell her she was a liar and a fake unless she settled down with us. Finally, she stopped coming back. That's why I needed to find her. If I could just explain — they meant well, they didn't understand she was different — maybe she'd forgive us. Or take me with her."

Jaz shook her head. She rubbed a hand across her wet cheeks and stood suddenly. "Wait here a second." She hurried into the basement.

Bracken shivered. His back was wet. He lifted a hand from the floor, found it was wet, and looked down to see he was sitting in a pool of… something.

The lights above the workspace came on, glowing a gentle orange-yellow. Janus appeared behind the counter, moving about. The running faucet went silent; the dishwasher door closed. Janus glanced at Bracken and smiled, as if nothing were out of the ordinary. "Evening. Or morning, rather."

Bracken looked back down at the floor. Now he could see that he was sitting in blood. He stood quickly, reeled, and caught himself on the edge of the nearest counter.

Jaz came back upstairs clutching a wide, thin, hardback book to her chest. She glanced at Janus as she came around the counters and her eyes narrowed, but for once she didn't yell at him to go away. She caught Bracken's arm and helped him onto a stool. He sat stiffly, holding his arms away from his body.

Jaz laid the book on the counter in front of him. On the cover was painted a pair of brown, feathered wings.

"This is a book," Jaz said, as Bracken stared at the cover.

"I know what a book is," Bracken replied, feeling sticky and gross. He wondered if it was possible to bathe in a coffee shop.

"It's Sadie's. She wrote it."

"She did?" Bracken leaned forward and touched the cover, running his fingertips along the edge of the book and then over the wings. Then he snapped his fingers away as the wings faded, sinking down into the white background. Black and gold letters faded in, one line appearing at a time, as if they were being drawn by an invisible pen: The Brown Bird and the Trickster King. The wings faded back in on either side of the words, fluttering slowly. Bracken exclaimed and picked up the book with both hands. He ran his fingers over the animated wings, but felt only the flat, smooth surface of the cover.

"Open it," Jaz prompted.

Bracken set the book down on the counter and opened it, turning over the first page. It was slightly glossy, cream-colored, and blank. Jaz reached over and drew her fingertip across the paper.

A watery, painted image of a brown bird surfaced and moved across the page, wings pumping in flight. It traveled across the left-side page, dipping into the crevice made by the book's spine and onto the right-side page, where a spread of tall, white-tipped mountains rose to block the bird's path. Black script appeared along the bottom of the scene:

*'Once, there was a brown bird who loved
to travel. She decided to leave home and
fly to a new land she had never seen,
beyond the great Snowy Mountains…'*

Bracken looked up at Jaz. "I know this story. She used to tell it to us when she visited."

Jaz smiled. "I know. She had this book made in Vasencea. Davin—"

"Was helping her, yeah." Bracken turned to the next page, which was also blank until he brushed a fingertip across it. More illustrations surfaced: The brown bird attempting to fly over an icy summit and failing, returning to the green earth in lament. "How does it do that?"

"It's self-animating paper. They make it in Vasencea with alchemy. It works like oil on water, except rather than floating on top, the color pigments stay beneath the fibers of the paper until touch activates them." Jaz watched the moving bird fluttering, straining against a wind too strong for it. "It was a gift for you."

Bracken forgot about being bruised and sticky with his own blood. He stared at Jaz, forgetting even to breathe.

She met his eyes, for once not turning away. "This was the last thing she wanted to do before she died. She wanted to go see you, Bracken. She just… ran out of time. And I should have sent it to you. I kept telling myself I would, but I... I was afraid you'd figure out the truth and come here and end up wasting your life here too." Jaz made a sound in her throat that was half sob, half laughter. "But you came anyway."

Bracken almost put an arm around her, but Janus was lurking at the counter nearby, watching. Plus, he had a vague feeling that if he gave in to his impulse to comfort her, he would have to forgive her, and if he forgave her they would really, actually become friends. If they became friends, any agreement with Janus would be out of the question since he was technically an enemy. And Janus was his last remaining hope of ever seeing Sadie again.

Bracken slid off his stool and closed the book, clutching it against his chest. His legs wobbled as he walked to the basement door, but he didn't stop until he had escaped to his room, just as the tears he'd been holding back streamed down his cheeks.

37

Coffee Ninjas

It was a beautiful story. Bracken read it when he finally woke up, curled on his side on the cot. He turned the pages slowly, savoring each illustration and word. He remembered the story from when Sadie used to tell it, but she had expanded on it since then, merging it with the story about the blue-haired princess. Now that Bracken knew the story behind the story, as it were, he could see why she had merged the two into one.

He was thirsty, his throat dry and lips tight, but he continued to read. In the end, the bird traded her wings, her ordinary, non-magical wings, for a key that would free herself and the princess from the box. Bracken had to brush his hand across his eyes every few moments to clear away the tears blurring his vision as he read. The illustrations moved scratchily over the last page: The princess distraught because the bird could no longer fly, and the bird overjoyed to finally be able to free the princess:

'Don't worry,' the bird told the princess.
'When we're free I'll just ride on your shoulder.'

Bracken had to push the book aside. His tears were falling too fast, and he didn't want to ruin the pages. He curled over his knees, shoulders shaking with emotion. This was why she'd left, and why she'd stayed away. Not for flightiness, not to escape a family that should have treated her better, but for loyalty. She'd gone to help a friend.

After a while, Bracken leaned back against the wall, gasping softly for air and rubbing his arm across his damp face. He pulled the book back onto his lap, and read again from the beginning. He read and reread the story, turning the pages back and forth to admire the moving artwork.

He only stopped when his thirst grew too strong to ignore. His limbs were stiff and cramping, his body demanding hydration.

He finally ventured upstairs, parched and sluggish, not bothering to texturize, but at least composed enough for conversation.

Vivid afternoon sunlight oozed into the shop, adding a glow to everything it touched. The chairs and tables were returned to their normal places, and Jaz had cleaned the floor. The spare suitcases were also gone, no doubt stored in the basement until they could be returned to their owners in a week. Outside, the brick landing pad and the city of Vasencea had been replaced by a wide paved street lined with low, white houses with red tile roofs. The roofs peaked sharply in the middle and curled up at the eaves, like tall red hats. Short trees with delicate, whiplike branches stood in front of the houses. A soft breeze occasionally rippled the bright yellow leaves.

Jaz turned as Bracken sidled onto the nearest stool. She looked tired, her eyes and mouth tight with hidden worry. "I was just about to check on you," she said, coming over. "How are you feeling?"

"Sore," Bracken replied. "It's too bad I don't reset like you."

Jaz picked up a teapot. "Want some? Tea is good for healing."

Bracken shook his head. "Just a gallon or so of water please."

Jaz poured him a glass of water, which needed refilling twice before he slowed down to sip on a fourth.

"Where are we now?"

"Kysoto," she answered.

Bracken couldn't remember reading anything about a Kysoto. Probably because he had stopped reading the binders once he found Vasencea. The coffee manual sat near the register; Bracken stretched an arm across the workspace to grab it.

Jaz began to say more, but stopped as Janus appeared on a stool beside Bracken.

"So, you were unable to find any information about Sadie's whereabouts in Vasencea," said Janus, watching Bracken retract his arm with the notebook in tow.

Jaz made a small, irritated noise in her throat and went back to arranging spoons and glasses on the espresso counter.

"It's too bad I didn't." Bracken flipped through the manual, searching for information on Kysoto. "Especially since Jaz says I have to go home tomorrow."

"Even though Jaz doesn't wish you to remain, I could still use you." Janus's smile seemed out of place beneath his inhuman eyes.

Bracken avoided looking straight at them. "Right. To help you get free."

Janus nodded. "You can still be united with your aunt. Even though she will be slightly different from the Sadie you knew, in time you will not notice. New memories will overtake the old."

Bracken thumbed the edge of the manual, fanning the worn pages. He waited for Jaz to yell at Janus, but she kept her back to them.

"You should hurry and decide," Janus prompted. "You don't have much time left."

"Until what? Monday?" Bracken looked over as the doors opened and stiffened.

Costello walked toward them, wearing loose black clothes, holding a black scarf in one hand.

Bracken gripped the edge of the counter. "Jaz, you said this wasn't—" He stopped.

Jaz was smiling.

"Hello, Kumosan," she said to Costello.

"Good morning, Jaz-san." Costello-Kumosan bowed prayerfully, pressing the scarf between his palms. He climbed onto the stool in front of the empty row of cups. Bracken gaped. The voice was Costello's, as well as the face and body. His eyes had the same piercing confidence, his jaw just as solid and manly, but there was no bluster or bullying, no shouting or shooting of air bullets.

"What are we tasting today, Jaz-san?" asked the new, improved Costello.

"I have three coffees. Two with spice notes and one — if I did it right — with toasted marshmallow. You all get to help me pick a holiday roast to feature."

"With great pleasure," said Costello-Kumosan. He noticed Bracken staring at him and nodded pleasantly. "Greetings. Are you here for the cupping ceremony?"

Bracken said, "No... yes. Kind of."

Janus leaned in and said softly, "Not to worry. He is simply an alternate version of the Costello you encountered yesterday."

"So… there are two of them."

"Many more than two," Janus corrected.

Bracken continued to stare. "What is he wearing?"

"Work clothes. He's an assassin."

"Is he going to shoot me again?"

"No. He doesn't know you, or anything his alternate does. The only thing they have in common is they look the same. Also, he only kills dictators."

"Does Kysoto have surplus of dictators?"

"They are always popping up, here and there. I think they're simply spawned in tanks and shipped off to take over cities. Eventually they get assassinated by the ninjas, and replaced, and so on."

"Sounds like a racket," said Bracken.

Janus shrugged and sipped his coffee. "Whoever organizes the coups and assassinations profits enormously from it, I'm sure."

"Who's behind it all?"

"It hardly matters," Janus said dismissively.

"Yeah, but it's interesting…"

Two more men dressed in the same black outfits entered. They greeted Jaz respectfully and settled at the counter with Kumosan.

Jaz returned their greetings and turned to Bracken. "They're here to taste coffee. We do it every Sunday."

She smiled as she said this, not her short smile but a long one, the same one she had given Sean when he complemented her roasting methods.

"Wow, Jaz. Coffee appreciation really is the way to your heart," observed Bracken.

"I'm just happy someone else appreciates it," she said pointedly, turning back to address Kumosan. "Where is Weisan? He's usually the first one in."

"Weisan has gone on his final mission," said Kumosan reverently.

"Oh." Jaz turned away, somewhat deflated.

Bracken leaned in to Janus to ask softly, "What does that mean?"

"He died attempting to assassinate the latest dictator."

Jaz gripped the edge of the counter with both hands, staring down at her knuckles.

"He was ready to give his life for his people since the day he was born," recited Kumosan.

Jaz blinked hard several times before turning and opening the dishwasher. "I'll miss him."

"Do not worry, Jaz-san. He will respawn until he completes his mission. It is the ninja way." Kumosan nodded.

"Whenever one of you respawns I never see him again. It's the same to me as if you died."

Bracken felt a twinge of sympathy for her. He wouldn't have believed it before last night, but now he knew that

Jaz actually did care what happened to the people in the worlds outside of her shop, in her own way.

"Have hope," Kumosan was saying. "We will assassinate the despot who oppresses your city. It is our destiny."

"It's not my city." Jaz shut the dishwasher harder than necessary. Then she changed her tone and said brightly, "Let's begin, shall we?"

38

Timeline Trouble

Strangely, a cupping didn't include actually drinking coffee but soaking grounds in cups of hot water and slurping the brew from a spoon. This seemed to be the elitist way to experience coffee. They discussed tasting notes and flavor profiles, leaning over a paper with color-coordinated adjectives arranged in concentric circles, using words like 'acidity' and 'mouth-feel' and 'tannins.' They agreed that one coffee had a wonderful pecan aroma but lacked body, and criticized the grassiness of another. Bracken watched them, quietly sipping his water, until the glass was empty and his attention had dwindled to nothing. He flipped through the pages of the coffee manual, looking for notes written by Sadie. The page titled 'Ninjas' was suddenly relevant. It had several entries. One, in Sadie's neat handwriting, was contemplative:

When I asked her about it, Jaz couldn't say whether the zealous ninjas respawned or not, but there are an awful lot of them, and always new ones coming into the shop. They might be reincarnations of their past selves, or clones, or who knows what, but when a ninja dies, they are lost to her. None ever recognize her, or have any prior memories of her. The rate at which she makes friends here and loses them is far greater than all the other worlds combined.

Dictators and tyrants spawn as fast as the ninjas. Ninjas are trained from birth to assassinate the dictators, as dictators are raised from birth to oppress cities and eventually be assassinated. Despicable as the order of things here might be to Jaz, she knows interference is pointless if not impossible. Regardless, it bothers her deeply.

Bracken looked up and stared at the windows, imagining what it had been like for Sadie, spending a quiet Sunday with Jaz and the ninjas. Perhaps she had written this very passage at the counter where Bracken sat, sipping coffee, listening to the technical coffeespeak, perhaps joining in.

He could almost see Sadie behind the counter, working the register while Jaz made drinks. Explaining the difference between roast flavors. Talking Jaz down from attacking customers. Eating pastries in the morning, ordering from a different restaurant every night.

He could almost hear her voice.

Almost.

Janus cleared his throat, bringing Bracken's attention back to the shop. Jaz was loading cups into the dishwasher. The ninjas had all gone.

"Bracken…"

Bracken shook himself and blinked. He stared at Janus, then over to Jaz. "I'll think about it."

"Don't take too much time deciding. I have all the time in eternity, but you do not."

Bracken opened his mouth to respond, but the sound of another voice stopped him. A female voice, belonging to a lovely creature with a short skirt and striped stockings who appeared to be a Morpha. She was talking quietly to Athamas, who strode coolly beside her, his long coat feathering slightly along its edges.

Bracken blinked several times, rubbed his eyes and blinked again. He turned to Janus. "Did they just walk in through that window?"

But Janus had disappeared.

Bracken blinked again and looked to Jaz.

She froze for a moment, watching them approach the counter. She glanced at Bracken, a flash of anxiety crossing her face. Then she breathed in sharply and said to Athamas, "When you see Weisan tell him 'I told you so.'"

"I already have. He said he'll get them next time," Athamas replied.

Corrine scoffed, hopping onto a stool. "Yeah, right. You know how many the ninjas lost this month? Thirteen. Dictators lost four. Ninjas need better drafting next month."

"She's not the one to tell, Corrine," said Athamas, glancing at Bracken as he sat. He quickly stood again, looking sharply at Jaz. "Jaz. What did you do?"

Jaz was suddenly occupied looking through the pastry case for blueberry cobbler.

Athamas turned stiffly to Bracken. "What are you doing here? Keep in mind it is within my discretion to terminate threatening anomalies ahead of schedule."

It was Bracken's turn to stare. On his last visit, Athamas had been focused on sending Fatson to some purgatory. But now all that focus was on Bracken. His mind went numb. He tried to say something, but he could only think of the hole in his chest, of blacking out and then waking up soaked in his own blood.

"It was an accident..." Jaz defended weakly.

Athamas produced a worn black notebook from inside his coat and flipped through it with intense concentration.

Then he sighed deeply. "Now the date is going to be off."

Corrine scoffed. "No, the date just looks off. It will look right in the base timeline in his world. It was the same with Sadie. When she traveled in here, her date jumped all over the place, but it always went back to normal when this place stopped in her world. If you did this electronically you could program some equation for this, you realize."

"I don't need equations. The book is right. He's wrong." Athamas jabbed the notebook toward Bracken's chest with a scowl. "What did you do?"

Jaz hopped over the counter, sliding across to drop down on the other side by Athamas. "It… there was an accident, and he got hurt…"

Athamas wasn't listening. He studied the notebook again, one dark eye twitching, then shoved the book at Corrine. "Find an equation for this."

Corrine stretched onto her tiptoes to look at the pages, and raised an eyebrow. "Shoot, kid…"

"What's it say?" Bracken leaned across the counter to see the book.

Athamas pulled it from his view. "Tomorrow. And also yesterday. In the base timeline, you would have succumbed tomorrow. In this timeline, you would have died yesterday."

Jaz had gone quite still. "Athamas."

Athamas stared hard at the page. Then he turned to study Bracken. "The timeline changed from the base timeline when he entered here, and now it has changed again. What was to happen will no longer happen at the proper time." He thrust a long finger at Bracken. "You made an agreement with one of them. I recognize their work."

He didn't have to say Lumenatra; everyone in the room knew the implication, even Bracken.

"I'm... supposed to die tomorrow?" Bracken felt lightheaded. He steadied himself with a hand on the counter.

"Since you are now a free-roaming anomaly, you can be terminated immediately," said Athamas.

"What?" Bracken's steadying hand clamped down on the counter edge while he scanned the room, bracing for a dark, birdlike shadow to appear and slice him with its beak.

"Athamas, no." Jaz stepped in front of Athamas, forcing him to meet her eyes. "It wasn't him. I made the agreement on his behalf."

Bracken stared at her. "You made an agreement? With who, Janus?"

Jaz nodded.

"But...I thought the shop only revives you."

"It does. But remember how Sadie didn't seem to age? That was the shop. It does have a healing effect on those who travel in it. And Janus has the power to advance time in the shop, so I had him..."

For some reason, tears stung Bracken's eyes. "You did that for me?"

"Janus did. I just… insisted."

"How could you do such a thing?" Athamas growled, pulling her attention back to him. "You are here because of a previous agreement you made!"

"I couldn't let him die!" Jaz cried. "He's Sadie's nephew."

"Sadie never caused such trouble. When he reenters his home world, he can cause things to happen that wouldn't had he died at the proper time!" Athamas' voice went from stern to angry, its resonance filling the room.

Jaz flinched, but stood her ground. "He's not going to cause anything to happen. He's going to go home."

"He was supposed to die tomorrow, Jaz. What if he goes home and the next day he shoots someone who's supposed to die in forty years?"

"He's not going to shoot anyone!"

Corrine lounged against the counter, resting on both elbows. "The Lumenatra jack with probabilities all the time, Athamas. Just look at this shop. That book will never be a hundred percent accurate because of them. You have to let some of this slide."

Bracken's head was spinning, trying to grasp the nature of the conversation. "So was I supposed to die yesterday, or tomorrow?"

"You won't die tomorrow, that's the point," Corrine said.

Athamas straightened. "If an anomaly is deemed a big enough threat I—"

Jaz stepped closer, laying a hand on his arm. "Please, Athamas. Don't."

Athamas looked down at her. "Why does it concern you so much?"

Jaz flinched again. "He's… my friend."

Bracken swallowed, his chest suddenly tight as his mind flashed back to the previous night, of refusing to admit the same. "Look. Why don't I just stay with Jaz in The Defiant? Then I can't go out and shoot someone, and mess up the balance or whatever."

Athamas stiffened. "Because there's nothing forcing you to stay here like Jaz. Sadie went with me willingly when her time came, but you are nothing like her. Do you know how many people die every second? How many I am talking to this very instant? Tell me why you, out of all of them, should be an exception?"

Bracken opened his mouth to answer, and suddenly couldn't. Because Athamas was right. He was nothing like Sadie.

Even knowing what hell Jaz was enduring in this prison disguised as a café, knowing she had gone out of her way to protect him, even saved his life knowing he would probably abandon her for a promise of finding some version of his aunt — which in itself was shameful enough — he was at that moment *still* considering doing exactly that.

Which made him even more ashamed.

"Because…" He finally managed to say, "Because I'm going to help her escape."

39

Delayed Departure

"Bracken," Jaz began, shaking her head.

"Do you know how much this place is wearing her down?" Bracken wasn't sure Athamas understood how much, even if he did care. "She can't even remember what's in her own basement or what she did last month. She has projects down there she probably doesn't even remember starting. All just to keep herself sane, because she knows she might never leave. Sadie knew it too. That's why she stayed. It's what friends do."

"How many friends do you think Athamas and I have?" Corrine had pulled a napkin to her and was doodling on it with a pen she'd produced from somewhere. She paused to glance over at Bracken. "Everyone we interact with except for Jaz is dead or dying. Not much potential for relationships there."

"Athamas, please. Don't take him," Jaz said quietly.

Athamas faced her, his expression mingled sternness and sympathy. "Even if I don't today, he will still eventually die. Like Sadie. The one after him will die too, and the next. You are setting yourself up for an even more painful cycle."

Jaz bowed her head and leaned her forehead against his chest. "I know he'll have to go sometime. Just… don't take him now."

"You ask much of me."

She raised her eyes, and a look passed between them, the same as when they'd last seen each other. Fondness. Hunger. Longing. She wanted death as much as Death wanted to claim her.

Corrine tapped the counter with her knuckles and held the napkin up to Athamas. He took it and frowned. "Et tu, Corrine?"

Corrine shrugged. "It's not like we have a bunch of other people to talk with for any length of time."

"I will make a deal," Athamas said slowly. "Jaz's case can allow for some… exceptions. I will allow Bracken to live until his new date of expiration. With the understanding that if he begins to pose a threat to the expiration dates of others he will be terminated immediately, and this will be his fate." He held up the napkin to Bracken. Corrine had sketched a scenario that, to Bracken, was the worst way imaginable to die. He stared at it, a chill streaking through his body.

"I know it's a bit extreme, but this is what you ask for," Athamas said.

Bracken had to swallow a dry spot growing in his throat. "I'll be careful, then."

"You agree to the terms?"

"I agree."

Jaz sighed softly, as if tension were going out of her.

"Very well." Athamas folded the napkin and put it in his pocket. He looked from Jaz to Corrine. "Are you ladies happy now?"

"Thank you," Jaz said softly.

Corrine simply shrugged, but Bracken thought he saw a pleased quirk on her lips.

"Then we should go," Athamas said. "There's a death match tournament starting in Makamit."

Jaz watched them leave, then looked at Bracken. But now it was he who couldn't make eye contact.

He turned away from her and went downstairs. He knew who would be in his room, waiting, but he still started at the sight of Janus sitting on the cot.

"That was a lucky escape." Janus crossed one leg over the other, resting his hands on his knee. "Death doesn't just make an exception for anyone."

Bracken stopped in the doorway, watching him. "Do you ever intervene for people just because? Or does someone always have to make a deal with you first?"

"Whatever happens out there has no bearing on what happens to me. To try and right every wrong would be madness."

"It's just not your problem, you mean." Bracken went to the cot and retrieved the picture book from atop his pillow, taking several steps back as soon as he had it

Janus leaned forward and set his hands on either side of him on the mattress. "Think what good will come of us working together. You could be with your aunt again *and* help Jaz be freed from this place. You have nothing to lose and so much to gain."

Bracken shook his head. "I can't make a deal with you, Janus."

Janus' expression did not change, but something about him suddenly felt tense. "No?"

"I already made a deal with Athamas. I have to behave myself, which means I can't do anything that would put another world in danger. Like set you free." Bracken raised his shoulders and hands in a 'what can you do' gesture.

Janus went very still. He resembled a statue more than a living person. But something… dark radiated from his eyes. Not a color, exactly, and not an emotion. Just a feeling. Black rage. "You'll change your mind, after enough time passes. When you're desperate enough. Even Jaz finally broke down, over you."

Bracken pushed down a rising chill and continued. "I'm going to find the doorway generator that Sadie was looking for. When I have it, I'm setting Jaz free."

Bracken turned his back, closing the door behind him as he walked out of the room. Even through the closed door, he could feel the Lumenatra's eyes watching him.

Jaz was sitting on the bottom of the basement stairs, her hands covering her mouth almost prayerfully. Bracken was sure she had heard everything.

She lowered her hands slowly. Some light filtered down from the door above, making her blue hair glow faintly. "What made you change your mind?"

Bracken shrugged, rubbing his neck as he glanced away. "I guess I realized you're right. Sadie was one of a kind. No one could replace her. And staying here with you was the best thing she could have done with her life. She believed that, and so do I."

Jaz smiled slowly. She stood and, putting her hands on his shoulders, leaned in and kissed his cheek.

He pulled back and rubbed at the spot. "C'mon, Jaz. Your boyfriends will get mad at me."

"Boyfriends?" She stepped back, making a face.

"Sean and Athamas."

"Athamas is not my boyfriend." Jaz turned and started back upstairs.

Bracken followed her. "He totally is…"

40

Monday, Again

Bracken sat at the empty counter, turned toward the windows to watch the sun rise over Homburg.

Jaz stood behind the espresso machine, fiddling with switches along its front. The refrigerators beneath the counters hummed, the espresso machine gurgled and swished as the boilers filled and heated. "I told your sister to check back here in the morning if she didn't find you. She should show up sometime soon." Jaz said. "Want some cobbler, for the road?"

"No thanks. I'm going to get some real food later." Bracken yawned and folded his arms across his backpack, which lay on the counter in front of him.

He and Jaz had stayed awake most of the night, looking at photos, talking, looking at more photos, eating pastries, and finally just sitting in the café in silence together. It felt like the hours before a long trip, a long separation.

"And there she is…" Jaz nodded toward the windows as Kajaani passed in front of them, heading toward the doors. "Not wasting any time, that one."

Bracken sighed and slid off his stool. "Well…"

They looked at each other across the counter.

"See you later."

"See you." Bracken gathered his backpack and went to meet his sister at the doors.

"Turn the sign around on your way out!" Jaz called after him.

Bracken did so, while Kajaani scowled at him through the glass, rubbing her black-and-red striped arms against a mild chill. Her unbrushed black hair flowed loosely to her shoulders, bristling in response to her mood.

Stepping outside felt strange. Cool air, heavy and green smelling, brushed softly against his skin. Sunlight glowed along Main Street, illuminating the brick buildings on either side of the road, all the way to the fields at the edge of town where Bracken had encountered the flash flood.

The previous day, and a week earlier.

Kajaani latched onto his arm with a vengeance. "Surprised to see me?"

Bracken shook his head. "Jaz told me you were in town."

She glared, digging her fingers in. "Yeah, to find you! Where's my camera?"

"Here." Bracken unzipped his backpack and produced the camera. "It needs more film. I, uh, used it all."

She took it, still glaring. "Why did you steal it anyway? I would have lent it to you. And what were you even *thinking*, running off like that? Mom and Dad are having fits—"

She broke off as Bracken suddenly hugged her.

"I'm sorry. I just… needed to know."

"Know what?" Kajaani pulled back and looked into his face, her anger giving way to concern.

"What happened to Sadie." He twisted to point behind him with his free arm. "She worked at The Defiant. The… ah, manager, Jaz. She told me all kinds of crazy stories about her."

"She didn't say anything about that to me." Kajaani turned to the windows thoughtfully. "Where is Sadie now then?"

Bracken swallowed. "She died. Right before my birthday. Jaz didn't have any way to contact us. And when you came last… yesterday… she was so surprised that she didn't say anything. Jaz isn't very good at showing emotion."

Kajaani lay a hand on his arm, this time gently. "What happened?"

"She… got sick. It was pretty sudden."

Kajaani nodded. She looked slightly relieved, as he knew she would. He pretended not to notice. She might never learn the truth, but he knew it. That was what mattered.

"She left something for us though." He reached into his backpack for the picture book.

Kajaani put an arm around his shoulders, guiding him down the sidewalk. "You can show me on the train home."

"Yeah, about that…"

*

Morphas masked in myriad shades of yellow filled The Defiant, circling tables and leaning against the counters. The sun cast down its own yellow hues, shifting from a bright neon morning to a smoldering golden evening. The shop grew quieter as customers went home for their meals.

Windows along the street shone with orange-yellow electric lights as Jaz cleared the final dishes from tables and loaded them in the dishwasher. She crossed the empty café to lock the doors, which had been propped open to let in the fresh air.

Bracken stood just outside them.

Jaz stopped at the threshold facing him and stared for a moment. She folded her arms. "No, Bracken. We've been through this. Go home, be good, don't cause trouble. Come visit me occasionally."

Bracken raised a hand. "Hear me out. I'll only travel with you one day a week. That's one day in seven by your time. The other days, I'll work at the café and leave when you close. I'll get a place to stay in Homburg the other days of the week."

Jaz considered this, chewing the inside of her cheek. "You'll still age too quickly—"

"It's my life, Jaz. I'd rather spend it here than anywhere else."

Jaz sighed and stepped aside. "Behave, or I'll ban you for life."

He walked into the café, grinning as he passed her.

Jaz pushed the doors closed and locked them. She stood a moment, her eyes distant, staring at his retreating reflection in the glass. A slow, happy smile crept over her lips. She reached up and turned the sign to 'closed.'

***

Acknowledgments

Special thanks to my writing partner of many years, a brilliant mad genius by the name of Jeremy Ledgerwood, who created the characters of Athamas and Corrine, allowed me to adapt them for this story, and who helped me develop ideas for the worlds The Defiant visits.

Thanks to my editor, Morgen Bailey, and to Justin Schut, who did the illustration of The Defiant used in the cover design. They made the finished book the best it could be.

Thanks to my better half, Jeremy Nelson, for lauging at my stupid jokes, and making sure I didn't quit.

Always thanks to Lauren Lantis, Elizabeth Moore and Brittany McFalls, my fellow baristas-in-crime, who made the bad moments in coffee survivable, and the good ones immortal.

About the Author

Jinn Nelson is a former barista currently living in Austin, Texas, with ambitions to move to a different dimension (once she finds a working portal) or, failing that, to somewhere in Ireland.

Traveler is the first of a trilogy, inspired by her time as a barista and fascination with the multiverse. For updates on future releases and to read her other works, visit www.JinnNelson.com.

Thanks for reading!
Remember to tip your barista.